More Praise for MaryJanice Davidson and Her Novels

"Delightful, wicked fun . . . Erotically passionate!"

—Christine Feehan

"Entertaining, wicked, and delightful."

—*Romance Reviews Today*

"A must-read for fans who appreciate a humorous out-of-this-world tale . . . fast-paced and filled with zingers."

—*Midwest Book Review*

"One of the funniest books I have ever read! MaryJanice Davidson has once again brought to life an independent, wisecracking heroine . . . The story is fast-paced, the sex is hot, and the humor outrageous! I highly recommend this story to everyone."

—*Paranormal Romance Reviews*

"Classic MaryJanice Davidson, in that it had me laughing throughout the book. It is one of the most original story ideas I have read in a long time also . . . [and] has the steamy love scenes that Ms. Davidson is known for . . . awesome."

—*The Best Reviews*

"[A] wickedly clever and amusing romp. Davidson's witty dialogue, fast pacing, smart plotting, laugh-out-loud humor, and sexy relationships make this a joy to read."

—*Booklist*

continued . . .

"A hilarious romp full of goofy twists and turns, great fun for fans of humorous vampire romance."

—*Locus*

"A bawdy, laugh-out-loud treat!"

—*BookPage*

"Smart, sarcastic, frequently profane, and maniacally inventive."

—*The Fort Myers (FL) News-Press*

"[A] hilarious, outrageous romp that . . . has more than one unexpected twist."

—*Library Journal*

Titles by MaryJanice Davidson

UNDEAD AND UNWED
UNDEAD AND UNEMPLOYED
UNDEAD AND UNAPPRECIATED
UNDEAD AND UNRETURNABLE
UNDEAD AND UNPOPULAR
UNDEAD AND UNEASY

DERIK'S BANE
DEAD AND LOVING IT
SLEEPING WITH THE FISHES
SWIMMING WITHOUT A NET
DEAD OVER HEELS

CRAVINGS
(with Laurell K. Hamilton, Rebecca York, Eileen Wilks)

BITE
(with Laurell K. Hamilton, Charlaine Harris, Angela Knight, Vickie Taylor)

MYSTERIA
(with P. C. Cast, Gena Showalter, Susan Grant)

DEMON'S DELIGHT
(with Emma Holly, Vickie Taylor, Catherine Spangler)

Dead Over Heels

MaryJanice Davidson

BERKLEY SENSATION, NEW YORK

THE BERKLEY PUBLISHING GROUP
Published by the Penguin Group
Penguin Group (USA) Inc.
375 Hudson Street, New York, New York 10014, USA
Penguin Group (Canada), 90 Eglinton Avenue East, Suite 700, Toronto, Ontario M4P 2Y3, Canada (a division of Pearson Penguin Canada Inc.)
Penguin Books Ltd., 80 Strand, London WC2R 0RL, England
Penguin Group Ireland, 25 St. Stephen's Green, Dublin 2, Ireland (a division of Penguin Books Ltd.)
Penguin Group (Australia), 250 Camberwell Road, Camberwell, Victoria 3124, Australia (a division of Pearson Australia Group Pty. Ltd.)
Penguin Books India Pvt. Ltd., 11 Community Centre, Panchsheel Park, New Delhi—110 017, India
Penguin Group (NZ), 67 Apollo Drive, Rosedale, North Shore 0632, New Zealand (a division of Pearson New Zealand Ltd.)
Penguin Books (South Africa) (Pty.) Ltd., 24 Sturdee Avenue, Rosebank, Johannesburg 2196, South Africa

Penguin Books Ltd., Registered Offices: 80 Strand, London WC2R 0RL, England

This book is an original publication of The Berkley Publishing Group.

This is a work of fiction. Names, characters, places, and incidents either are the product of the author's imagination or are used fictitiously, and any resemblance to actual persons, living or dead, business establishments, events, or locales is entirely coincidental. The publisher does not have any control over and does not assume any responsibility for author or third-party websites or their content.

Copyright © 2008 by MaryJanice Alongi
Excerpt from *Undead and Unworthy* copyright © 2008 by MaryJanice Alongi
Cover art by Stanley Chow
Cover design by Lesley Worrell
Text design by Tiffany Estreicher

All rights reserved.
No part of this book may be reproduced, scanned, or distributed in any printed or electronic form without permission. Please do not participate in or encourage piracy of copyrighted materials in violation of the author's rights. Purchase only authorized editions.
BERKLEY SENSATION is a registered trademark of Penguin Group (USA) Inc.
The "B" design is a trademark belonging to Penguin Group (USA) Inc.

First edition: March 2008

Library of Congress Cataloging-in-Publication Data

Davidson, MaryJanice.
Dead over heels / MaryJanice Davidson.— 1st ed.
p. cm.
ISBN 978-0-425-21941-6
1. Werewolves—Fiction. I. Title.
PS3604.A949D436 2008
813'.6—dc22 2007046407

PRINTED IN THE UNITED STATES OF AMERICA

10 9 8 7 6 5 4 3 2 1

This anthology is dedicated to the victims of the I-35 bridge collapse in Minneapolis. My cousin missed it by an hour, for which I give thanks every day. And my heart breaks for those who did not.

This will be the third time I've had to rewrite a novella/novel due to current events. One of my heroines was stabbed by a manta ray (as was the late Steve Irwin), and originally Betsy and Sinclair were going to spend their honeymoon stopping a nasty-bad vampire from blowing up the Brooklyn Bridge (the third is too embarrassing to get into, so I'll save that for another time).

I'm either getting psychic in my old age, or there's nothing new under the sun. Either way, my editor has to pay the price ("Hi, yeah, I have to completely rewrite the last hundred pages of the novella you're waiting for so it's going to be late—don't hang up!") and has never said so much as a bad word to me, no matter how often I must rewrite history, or how late the manuscript is as a result.

During one of our P.R. meetings, my rep asked after the

Brooklyn Bridge story. “Well, I can’t do it now,” was my reply. “And it’s a real shame I have to rewrite . . . and not just from a personal standpoint.”

“Creepy,” was my friend Jessica’s comment, and I couldn’t demur.

So this book is for her, too. Many thanks, Cindy Hwang. And many thanks to those employees at Berkley whose lives were made more difficult because I’m apparently seeing the future in my old age.

Contents

* * *

Undead and Wed: A Honeymoon Story

No man will ever bring out of that office the reputation which carries him into it . . . the honeymoon would be as short as in any other, and its moments of ecstasy would be ransomed by years of torment and hatred.

—THOMAS JEFFERSON

★

I do not want a honeymoon with you. I want a good marriage. I want progress, and I want problem solving which requires my best efforts and also your best efforts.

—GERALD FORD

★

Too fucking busy, and vice versa.

—DOROTHY PARKER,

in response to her editor's request for work on her honeymoon

Author's Note

The events of this novella take place a week after the events in *Undead and Uneasy.*

Prologue

"The king and queen are coming to New York."

The vampire, an ancient creature even by the standards of the undead, smiled. "Don't tease, Robert. It's so unkind."

"I'm not teasing, my dear one. They're coming. They'll be here the day after tomorrow."

"What fun!"

Although he had made this vampire, as he had made many others, he was a little afraid of it. "Or, we could leave town."

"Leave? This is our territory!"

"Yes, and since they took power, no one has been able to stand against The One and Sinclair."

"The One," the vampire scoffed. "Barely—what? Two years old? I don't believe she even exists."

"She killed Nostro," he said quietly. "And Marjorie."

"They were sloppy and complacent."

And we aren't? he thought but did not say.

"Someone killed them, but I'll believe in this The One nonsense when I actually see her. No, it's too too good. If I believed in such things I would say it's meant to be. The king! Coming here! Of all the places he could have chosen, he's coming *here*. Oh, I can't wait!" The creature frowned. "Robert, you don't seem terribly enthused."

Terribly terrified was more like it, but he had no intention of admitting that. Instead, he sighed soundlessly, without breath. "So I take it we aren't leaving town?"

Siamese blue eyes narrowed at him. "I will, of course, do as my sire commands."

But that was a lie. He wasn't in charge here, and they both knew it.

"Then we stay," he said, surrendering. And the thing he had made chortled and bounced and giggled, and he smiled at it, and hated it, but he loved it, too.

Because he had made it, all those years ago when there were more horses in Manhattan than automobiles.

Chapter 1

I was so excited to land at the airport in New York City (La Guardia or the other one . . . I wasn't paying attention to the pilot's intercom ramblings) that I didn't even bother with the stairs leading from the private plane to the ground. I just jumped, putting one hand on the railing and vaulting over, my black Gucci pumps dangling from my first two fingers. Didn't even feel the shock in my knees when I hit.

This was not a trick I could have pulled off while I was alive.

At the head of the stairs, my husband (husband! bridegroom! Yessssss!), Sinclair, king of the vampires, shook out the Wall Street Journal, folded it, and scowled down at me.

"How completely indiscreet, Elizabeth."

"Aw, Cooper doesn't care."

"Didn't see a thing, mum," Cooper assured me in his adorable Irish accent. He wasn't our pilot, and this wasn't our plane. It was my best friend, Jessica's. She'd lent it to us for our honeymoon, told us we could go wherever we wanted. Cooper had worked for Jessica for ten years and, as they say, knew where all the bodies were buried. "An' by the way, glad to see you're not dead. That was a nasty business a couple of springs back."

"Horrible practical joke," I said, referring to my firing, death, thirtieth birthday, and return from the grave as the long-foretold vampire queen. The people who *didn't* know I was a vampire either never knew I'd been killed, or thought it was a nasty trick thought up by my (late) evil stepmother. My friends and I did absolutely nothing to disabuse them of their silly-ass notions. "Really really bad taste. But it all worked out in the end."

"Yes indeed, mum," Cooper said, his blue eyes twinkling. Before Sinclair, I'd been a real sucker for Black Irish . . . that thick dark hair . . . those big blue eyes . . . umm . . .

Meanwhile, Sinclair (who wasn't Irish . . . in fact, I had no idea what he was) was gliding down the steps like a beauty queen (all he lacked was the tiara and bouquet of roses . . . and the tearful wave), when I knew perfectly well he could step off the IDS Tower and not even rumple his tie.

"Try to contain yourself," he sighed, moving past me toward the waiting limo.

"But it's New York City! And we're married! And we're in New York!" I, the country mouse, ran after him in my bare feet. I was wearing a sky blue shirt dress, no stockings. Oh, and my wedding ring! Not to mention my non cursed engagement ring. But that was a whole other story. "Don't you think it's going to be a blast?"

He muttered something that I, even with my super vampire hearing, couldn't catch. Probably just as well. Behind us, Cooper was calling, "See you in a week, mum! Sir!"

I flapped a wave over one shoulder and practically dived into the limo (fortunately, the door was being held open by the driver, a tall, lean, gorgeous black guy with cheekbones you could cut yourself on and the most amazing green eyes). Sinclair got in on the other side and shook out his paper once again.

"The Grange Hotel?" the driver asked.

"Yes," Sinclair replied absently as his pants made the dreaded *chirrup*. He fished out his cell phone, flipped it open, and blinked at the screen.

I sank back against the luxurious leather seats, halfway to full pout. "Don't even tell me. Tina called again."

"No matter where I am in the world," he reminded me mildly, "I still have business to attend to. And so do you."

"Dude! It's our honeymoon, all right? If that thing beeps in your pants one more time, I'm going to *eat* it, understand? Now shut the fucking phone, toss the fucking paper, and bask in our mutual love and joy, dammit!"

"I'm not sure *bask* is the verb I'd choose," he replied, but at least he put the phone away.

"Nice of Jess to arrange a limo," I commented, relieved to finally get a fraction of his attention. We'd been married for three whole days and I still couldn't believe it had really happened. Of course, according to my bridegroom, we'd been married since the first time we'd had sex. Don't even get me started. "It's not like her to throw her money around. And the plane! You believe she let us have her plane?"

"Point." Sinclair frowned. With his dark good looks, dark suit, broad shoulders, and strong jaw, he looked formidable anyway; when he wasn't smiling it was almost frightening. "She's the least pretentious billionaire I've ever known."

"Well, it's her dad's money."

He gave me a long look and I nearly drowned in those dark dark eyes. "Correction. He's dead. It's her money."

"Hwhuh?"

"It's. Her. Money," he repeated, well used to me being a little slow to pick up on current events.

I licked my lips. Jessica's dad was a touchy subject. Fucking incestuous greedy arrogant asshole; if he was alive, I'd kill him. Seriously. And I am not a girl who kills lightly, as anyone who knows me will totally understand.

"I mean, she doesn't consider it hers. It's not like she earned it. Hey, I'm not putting her down, but that's the way it is: she didn't earn any of it. That's why she doesn't throw it around, and that's why she has a day job."

Sinclair just looked at me. He knew me well enough to know when I wasn't coughing up the whole story. But in this case, it was just a theory. And the theory was, because Jessica had so recently (like, last week) recovered from terminal cancer, she was giddily celebrating life. (In all modesty, I must say that I cured her cancer. Yep. It's true. But that's a whole other story. Yay, me!)

"Including throwing planes and limos our way," I continued. "God knows what is going on in the mansion back home in St. Paul while we're away."

Never mind. I didn't want to know. I'd landed Sinclair—officially landed him, with paperwork and everything—and that was that. It was all I'd ever wanted, once I got over hating him and decided he was the vampire for me.

Sinclair, bless his cold, dead heart, tossed the newspaper on the floor and moved over until he was sitting beside me. He gave me a long, sweet kiss and cuddled me into his side. "Now, Mrs. Sinclair—"

"I told you, I didn't take your name!"

"—what would you like to do first?"

"I want to check into the hotel and have nasty kinky sex. Oh, and then go see a Broadway show."

"Odd," my husband commented. "I've never been alternately intrigued and terrified at the same time."

"Shut up. There's lots of good ones."

We discussed the pros and cons of live theater all the way to the hotel. I'd only seen high school stuff, and the plays at Chanhassen. And although those were pretty good, ergo Broadway would kick ass.

Sinclair, who had seen theater all over the world, begged to differ. And he did. Repeatedly. We had plenty of time, too, because even though it was full dark, traffic was horrendous.

And the *noise*. It sounded just as busy at ten o'clock at night as it would have during rush hour. And everything was open! Restaurants, convenience stores, shoe stores. It was unbelievable. New York City: the perfect tourist trap for vampires.

The limo driver pulled us right up to the front of the hotel, a forbidding stone building that looked like a transplanted castle. Sinclair helped me out (not that I needed it) while the driver shoved our luggage onto three bellboys.

Hand in hand, we swept into the lobby, me trying not to stare like I had cow shit on my heels, Sinclair looking perfectly at ease. He even yawned and, as we'd snacked on each other during the flight, didn't have to worry about showing fangs.

Finally, I thought, tightening my grip on his hand, a squeeze that would have broken the metacarpals of most people, *I get him to myself, and the Big Apple belongs to us. Oh, thank you, thank you Jesus.*

The month leading up to the wedding had been a frightening, lonely time for me and I was very glad to be reunited with my husband. Shit, I was glad he'd made the wedding at all. And now we were here, and I was going to make the most of it. Bet your ass.

Sinclair slammed to a stop so suddenly, and so gracelessly, that I plowed right into his back. "What's wrong?" I said into the cloth of his suit.

He muttered something, and I peeked around him.

Lounging across from the registration desk, taking up a small table in the bar area, was my best friend Jessica, and her boyfriend, Minneapolis Detective Nick Berry. They were both grinning at us with great big toothy smiles, at least one of which was fake.

"'Bout *time* you got here," Jessica said, and raised her Cosmo to me in a toast.

"Oh, fuck me," I groaned, surprised—but not in a good way.

"I don't see how we can fit that into the schedule now," my husband replied, looking as distressed as I've ever seen him.

Chapter 2

"Wow, great. This is great. Seriously. So great to see you. And what a great surprise! Now get out. Seriously."

"Awww, you know I'm your hero."

Sinclair was overseeing our luggage (as an alternative to strangling Jessica), Detective Nick was still in the lobby, and Jessica and I were arguing in the hallway outside our hotel room. It was a nice hallway . . . crimson carpet, gold wallpaper, gorgeous wall fixtures, dim lighting. Too bad I was so pissed it was totally wasted on me.

"You're not a tiny bit glad to see me?" Jessica was continuing.

I snapped my attention away from the wall fixtures. "Irrelevant! Now will you get lost already?"

"Don't you want to go shopping at Macy's with me?" Jessica had the nerve to sound wounded.

"We have one in the Mall of America," I said coldly. Also a Bloomingdale's and an Orange Julius. "And we've been a thousand times."

"Listen, Betsy . . ." Jessica was trying to look earnest, but as usual, her black hair was skinned back so tightly her eyebrows couldn't move. She could barely blink. Even in the low hallway lighting, her ebony skin shone, but not in a run-for-the blotting-papers way. She was, as usual, ridiculously beautiful, although still far too thin from the cancer. "I had to come."

"You had to crash my honeymoon?"

"You make it sound so mean."

I put my hands behind my back, because they wanted to fly up and fasten around my best friend's throat. "It *is* mean, you nimrod! I finally haul Sinclair's protesting ass to the altar—after rescuing him from certain death, *and* attending a double funeral, *and* taking on responsibility for BabyJon, *and* curing your cancer—and now here I am in New York City for the first time ever, ready to enjoy my honeymoon and you two idiots show up! No offense."

"Listen . . ." Wary of superior vampire hearing, Jessica tugged me by the elbow about ten feet further down the hallway. I didn't bother telling her Sinclair could still hear her from inside the room if he put his mind to it. Ears. Whatever. "I know it seems like a rotten trick—"

"'Oh, sure, Betsy, you guys can borrow my plane, but not until tomorrow . . .' Giving you plenty of time to beat us here." Now my hands wanted to fly into my hair and yank, hard. "And dumbass that I am, I actually left our contact information with you."

"Well, yes, but there was a method to my madness. You see, Nick hates you and Sinclair."

I blinked. "Yeah. So?"

"So?" Jessica threw her bony arms up in the air. "So? So I finally find a guy who doesn't give a shit that I gave away more money last year than the Target Corporation. So I finally find a guy who isn't so busy crushing on my best friend he doesn't even notice me. So I—"

"Hey, hey!"

"Oh, shut up, you know it's true. I finally find a guy who likes me for *me*, and it turns out he hates my best friend and her husband. Not 'God, they're boring, I hate going over there' hate, or 'I hate how all she talks about is shoes' hate. *Hate* hate. 'I hate war' hate. 'I hate plague' hate."

I blew out a breath, which wasn't necessary, but I'd only been dead a couple of years, and old habits died hard. Jessica wasn't lying, or even exaggerating. Her boyfriend did hate me, and it was a problem.

See, when I was a newborn vampire, out of my mind with the thirst, I'd feasted on Nick. And it . . . sort of drove him crazy. Crying, slobbering crazy. Sinclair had to step in and fix it by erasing Nick's memory of all events leading from my death.

We'd assumed it worked.

It hadn't.

It had actually worn off several months ago but, like all cops, Nick could lie like a sociopath. Instead he'd waited and watched. When Jessica had gotten sick, he'd explained in terrifying detail all the things he and his Sig Sauer would do to me if I didn't cure her. But I'd had plenty of other things on my mind at the time, and as upsetting as it was to find out how he really felt, there hadn't been much I could do about it.

Frankly, what with one thing and another (the aforementioned rescue, the wedding, Jessica's miracle cancer cure) I'd managed to put Nick's simmering hatred out of my mind.

"I can't have the man I love hating my best friend."

"So you figure we'll hang out on my honeymoon and get to be friends again?"

Jessica opened her mouth to reply, but our hotel door popped open and a bellboy (bellman, actually) trotted down the hallway toward us, dressed in the crimson uniform of the hotel staff. He was a wide-eyed redhead with a goatee. Goatees irritated me. Either shave it all off, or grow a proper, Grizzly Adams beard, that was my motto. "Mrs. Sinclair, did you want your shoes kept in the tissue paper, or—"

"It's *not* Sinclair and go away," I snapped, a little too forcefully, as all the expression fell out of his eyes and he spun jerkily around, hit the Exit door, and disappeared.

"Great, he's probably going to swan into the Hudson," Jessica said disapprovingly.

"The least of my problems," I snarled back, pretending I didn't feel hugely guilty. "Are you saying Nick thought coming to New York was a fine plan?"

"Well . . ."

I got it. "Ah. 'Hey, Nick, I've got a great idea for a way to mess with your archenemies . . . how about we beat them to their hotel and tag along on their honeymoon?'"

Jessica spread her hands and grinned the grin I could never resist. I ground my teeth in a vain attempt to resist. "He *did* smile. It's the first time I've seen him smile when you or Sinclair's names have come up. What could I do?"

The door opened again and Sinclair's head popped out, which was as startling as it sounds. "Where did the bellboy go?"

"Bellman," I said helpfully.

"I've got twenty pairs of shoes in here and I don't

know what you"—his eyes narrowed as he took in Jessica's grin—"I know that look. You're giving in, aren't you?"

"It's not like they're going to be sharing the room," I began, but my husband cut me off by shutting our door.

Great.

Jessica coughed. "Sorry," she almost whispered.

Chapter 3

Dinner was, um, an awkward affair. Nick was morbidly cheerful because he knew he was fucking with us, Jessica was trying to play peacemaker, I was as tense as a boiled cat, and Sinclair was icier than usual.

"Can I tempt you with the dessert specials?" our waiter asked, gliding by for the fiftieth time. He seemed to find us fascinating, and no wonder—we were giving off enough tension to light up the entire island of Manhattan.

"Sure," Nick said, grinning. He and Jessica had been the only ones to eat, of course, while Sinclair drank glass after glass of Cabernet and I worked my way through four peach daiquiris. "Run 'em by us."

"Well, we have a lovely crème brûlée—"

As opposed to a disgusting crème brûlée.

"—a flourless chocolate cake with mint hazelnut filling, a vanilla bean gelato, a peach tartin, and a miniature root beer float served in an espresso cup."

I burst out laughing.

"Careful, Minnesota," Jessica murmured, looking down at her napkin. "The straw in your hair is showing."

"I'll have the crème brûlée," Nick announced. "Money is no object—*he's* paying." Jerking a thumb in my husband's direction.

"Can I have the gelato except served as a milk shake?" I asked, when steel pincers clamped down on my forearm and I yelped.

"We are not lingering over this table."

"O-*kay*, can I have my arm back?"

"Mrs. Sinclair, do you want to press charges for spousal abuse?"

"Don't call me that, Nick, you rotten bastard, and I do not. I'll take that gelato to go," I added to the waiter, who was unabashedly goggling. And I'd always heard nothing fazed New York waiters.

"We'll take it in our room," Sinclair said shortly, standing. "Along with another bottle of the Cabernet. Charge the dinner to our room as well. Jessica. Detective Berry. Good evening."

And with that, I was unceremoniously hauled out of one of the toniest dining rooms in Manhattan. I would have given Sinclair a kick to the shins, except I caught a glimpse of Nick's nasty grin and decided I was more pissed at him than my husband.

Chapter 4

Our door had barely snicked shut when Sinclair started in. "This is intolerable and I will not—"

I decided to distract him the best way I knew how. I jumped on him, wrapping my arms around his neck and my ankles around his back. I pressed my mouth to his and licked his teeth. The alternative was engaging him in a lively discussion about that day's *Wall Street Journal*.

"Do not think," my husband gasped, as we staggered around the room together, knocking over lamps and pictures and such, "I am unaware of your motivation."

"Shut up and fuck me."

"Oh, I will. I just wanted you to understand I know what you're up to."

"Who cares? It's our honeymoon. Now boink!"

He snickered into my mouth. It always slew him when I used the *B* word.

"And stop laughing at me!"

"At once, my wife."

"You liar," I said, swallowing a giggle of my own.

He tugged at my clothes, and I tugged at his, and we got about two thirds naked and decided that was plenty. Then he was lowering me to the floor.

I couldn't stop kissing him; his mouth was original sin, and the wine had made his breath sweet and spicy, like the peach tartin I hadn't ordered. I couldn't blame him for rushing us out of there but I sure wish I'd been able to order dessert—*argh, focus, Betsy!*

Let's see, what's he doing? Oh, yes! We were more or less naked and I could feel his hands on my inner thighs, spreading my legs apart, could feel his sharp teeth on my tongue.

He entered me and I rose to meet him, pulling his shoulders, pulling him as close as I could. His hands were buried in my hair, pulling, stroking

O Elizabeth my Elizabeth I love I love I love

as we thrust against each other

And I love you Eric my husband my very own husband

and kissed and licked and bit.

love I love I love I love

I scrabbled to get even closer, bracing my legs against the wall

Oh Eric that feels so good don't stop don't stop don't WHAT THE HELL?

He stopped. And I was so surprised I barely noticed. "What's wrong?"

"I—" I was looking right at it and I still couldn't believe it. "I stuck my shoe in the wall!"

Carefully, he looked over his shoulder. My left leg was in the air (as was my right), but when I'd shifted to get better leverage, my super vampire strength had plunged the heel of my sandal right through the wall, where it stuck fast.

Sinclair looked back at me.

I tried to think of what to say. Stupid vampire strength! "I-I—"

Sinclair burst out laughing. I started to laugh, too, though I was slapping his shoulders and saying, "Stop it! Stop it! It's not funny! I can't get down! Help me, you asshat!" and in the end we left the shoe where it was, stuck about four feet up in the wall.

Chapter 5

We slept until sundown, and woke to a message from Jessica inviting us to the joint around the corner for dinner—her treat. Of course, since we couldn't eat solid food, we were cheap dates, but still. The offer was out there.

We debated it. "This is our honeymoon. It is time for you and I to spend alone."

"In a city of fifty million people?"

"Eighteen million," he said dryly. "All of whom are strangers."

I couldn't believe I was in the position of defending Jessica and Nick tagging along on our honeymoon. "Yeah, but think of Jessica's problem."

"I'm thinking," he said, "of my own."

"Yeah, yeah, but come on. Nick hates us, and she sees this as a chance for him to get over that."

"So we can all be one big happy family."

"Well. Yeah." We sort of were, usually . . . when we weren't in New York, a bunch of us lived in the same house in St. Paul. More or less happily. So it was really bugging me that Nick wasn't going along with the "come on, get happy" plan. I mean, it was bugging me now that Jessica had reminded me of the problem. "Exactly. Think of the position Jessica's in . . . if we don't fix this, she'll have to pick between me—I mean, us—and him."

"So?"

"Heartless bastard!" I cried, pounding on his (bare, yum!) chest with my fist.

"Jessica is a beautiful, intelligent, wealthy woman. She will have no trouble finding another boyfriend."

This just went to show how fucking little Sinclair knew about women in general and my friend in particular.

"She doesn't want another boyfriend, she wants Nick."

Sinclair sniffed.

"And you have to admit, this is sort of all our fault."

"We did what was necessary," he said with the cool arrogance of someone who'd been walking around on the planet for more than sixty years, "and would do it again. That doesn't mean we have to share every meal with them while we're honeymooning."

"Not every meal," I compromised.

He rolled his eyes and slipped on a shirt. I fought the urge to slip it back off. "As you wish," he said. "Not every meal."

"Yay! I mean, thanks."

He grunted.

"I'll call Jess."

He didn't bother with a grunt this time. I whipped out my phone and texted, "Dinner OK! See you at 8?"

A few seconds later my phone chirped at me. "8, OK!"

"We're on."

"Oh, splendid."

"Come on, it'll be—" *Fun*, I had been about to say,

which would only have been the biggest lie since "This won't hurt a bit." "Incredibly awkward and weird, but we can skip dessert again."

"Ah." He smiled at last and stepped into his boxer shorts . . . unfortunately. "A heroic sacrifice on your part, so I will say no more."

"Nobody loves a wiseass."

"Not true at all, my wife."

Chapter 6

It was, if possible, even worse than the evening before. Jessica was strained and smiled too widely, Sinclair had nothing at all to say, and Nick kept making needling remarks about our Revolting Army of the Undead.

I kept ordering daiquiris.

At least the waiter was nice, though he picked up on the tension and came over only when one of us obviously needed a refill or, in Jessica's case, more fries. I watched enviously as she plowed through a burger and fries and Nick chewed up a steak and a twice-baked potato. God, I missed solid food.

Finally, Nick pushed it too far with, "What's the matter, Vampire King? Am I raining on your parade? Tough to slip off and snack on civilians with a cop on your trail?" There was a muffled thump, and I knew Jessica had smashed her giant size-nine foot onto Nick's boot. Yee–ouch.

"So, anyway," I said, "no dessert for us, but thanks anyway."

"Once again you misunderstand my motivation, Detective Berry. If I seem terse it's not because you are intruding where you are obviously not welcome."

Oh, ouch, here we go.

"It's because at least half the staff of our hotel, and at least a third of the guests, are vampires."

I froze. Jessica froze. Nick froze. Sinclair drained his Merlot.

"Oh, fuck me," Nick said in a watery voice I'd never heard before. And I had a flash—most of Nick's fury was really fear.

"We're not in any danger," Jessica said firmly, and I could have hugged her. She had about nine yards of guts, and it had nothing to do with being rich. She was just brave. Brave and ballsy and loyal and if she wanted to tag along on my honeymoon to clear up some personal shit, was I going to get in her way? After she *hugged* me when I came back from the dead?

No.

"They're the king and queen of the vampires," she was telling Nick, who had turned as cheesy-pale as the beer he wasn't drinking. "None of them will touch us without their say-so. Although you're acting like such a prick, they just might sic one or two of them on us for the hell of it."

I stifled the impulse to cheer. Also, to rip Sinclair a new one for not mentioning that little factoid. "So when you planned our honeymoon, you picked Vampire Central?"

"Of course." He had the audacity to look surprised. "Where else would I choose? The staff can accommodate anything we wish. The Grange was a natural choice. Of course"—he gave Nick a heavy-lidded look—"I wasn't expecting company."

"*How* many of the staff?" Nick asked in a voice

that sounded like he was being strangled. "And which ones?"

"That," my husband replied, "I will not tell you."

Jessica and I looked at the men, then at each other. It was never much fun to watch a pissing contest, especially when the odds were so firmly stacked in one person's corner.

After a long, awful moment I said, "Jessica's right, Nick. We'd never let them hurt you."

"*You* didn't even know about them, you stupid bitch!"

"Nick!" Jessica gasped.

Sinclair's fist slammed on the table, which obligingly cracked. "Do not speak to my wife like that *ever again*."

"It's okay, don't fight, I've been called worse, *please* don't fight," I begged. "Let's just get the check and get out of here, okay? Oh, and, um, pay for the table."

"Go back to Vampire Central?" Nick cried, aghast.

"Well, there's a Hilton down the block."

"Hilton," Sinclair sneered. "Enjoy."

"What've you got against the Hilton corporation?" I cried. "Besides them, you know, spawning Paris and all."

"Isn't that more than enough?"

"*I've* had more than enough," Jessica snapped. "Check, please!"

Chapter 7

We'd barely gotten down the block when we saw the flashing lights and crowd.

"Uh-oh," Nick said. "Crime scene."

"The perfect end to a perfect evening," Sinclair muttered.

"You guys stay here. I'm gonna check it out."

"You're a little out of your jurisdiction!" I called after him. "Like, by two thousand miles!"

"Fifteen hundred," Sinclair and Jessica said in unison.

"You know, now that he's gone, how much longer are you going to let him torture us?"

"I'm sorry," Jessica said at once. "I guess this is turning out to be a pretty crummy idea. I just thought—I don't know what I thought." She cleared her throat. "You, uh, *will* mention to the staff not to snack on us, right?"

"There's an old vampire saying," I told her. "Don't shit where you eat."

"Ah, yes, that old vampire saying," Sinclair said, smiling for the first time since the waiter took our order.

We chitchatted for another minute or two, and then Nick came trotting back. "There's a dead kid in that alley," he said, almost snarling. "And if he's more than thirteen I'll eat the candles on his last birthday cake. So which one of you two dead assholes just couldn't wait for a little snack? Huh? Or did you team up on the poor kid? Did you—"

I slapped him. The sound was almost inaudible with all the background noise. One thing about New York I'd never get used to. All the noise. "That is enough, Nicholas J. Berry! You know Goddamned well I wouldn't do that and neither would Sinclair. I know you're pissed at us and I understand that, but there's pissed and there's ugly, and I've had enough of your ugliness. You don't want to be here? Get the fuck lost. If you *are* going to be here, watch your fucking mouth."

He didn't say another word all night.

Chapter 8

He couldn't," Jessica said the next night. "His jaw was numb for *hours* afterward. No feeling at all. I tried to talk him into going to the E.R. but he wouldn't do it. I was afraid you'd broken his jaw. But you just bruised the hell out of it."

"Oh my God," I said, appalled. I'd only been awake for about twenty minutes and she dropped *this* on me. "I didn't mean to hurt him! That much."

She shrugged. "He didn't exactly *not* have it coming. It's so hard to defend your boyfriend when he's being an unreasonable dick."

Tell me about it, I almost said, but managed to bite my tongue in time. Instead I yawned and jumped out of the bed.

"I don't know why you bothered to pack clothes at all," my friend snarked, eyeing my naked form.

"Stop me if you've heard this before, but it *is* my honeymoon."

"Where's Sinclair?"

"Dunno. But I'm betting he's conducting a private investigation about the dead kid. You know we'd never, and I know we'd never, but victims like that make us all look bad. Although I love how Nick gets all high and mighty, pretending ordinary humans don't pull this shit every damn d—" I closed my mouth with a snap; I'd almost broken Rule Number One: Do Not Shit On Your Best Friend's Honey.

She was nice enough to ignore my blunder. "And what's this shoe doing sticking out of the wall?"

I ignored *that*. "How'd you get in here, anyway?"

"Huh? Oh. Sinclair let me have his spare key. Said he didn't need one."

"He did?" Of course he did. He didn't have a problem with Jessica. "You'll, uh, keep that tidbit to yourself, right?"

She gave me a look of such scorn, my eyebrows nearly scorched.

"O-*kay*, don't look at me like that." I yawned and scratched. "I guess I better get dressed."

"Please," Jessica begged. "And leave your armpit alone; you look like an ape when you do that. A tall, blond, vampiric ape."

"I cannot believe the shit I've had to eat, and I've only been awake for five minutes! Leave that alone," I added, because Jessica was tugging at the shoe in the wall.

"It won't budge," she gasped. "What did you do?"

"Some things will never be told." I opened the door, put a firm hand in the middle of her back, and pushed. "Later, gator."

The door had no sooner shut when it opened, and my husband (would I ever get tired of that phrase? prob'ly not) stood in the doorway.

"Ready for our big day?" I asked.

"I'd rather," he replied, eyeing me up and down,

"stay in tonight and discuss world politics while chewing on your labia."

"That's . . . sweet. But you promised."

He sighed, which was unnecessary for a vampire. I guess his old habits died hard, too. "Let me see the list again."

This was a stall technique, since I knew full well he remembered all the stuff I wanted to do. Still, I obligingly dug in my purse and extracted an index card, on which I'd scrawled all the tourist-type things I wanted to do today: the Empire State Building, the Statue of Liberty . . . like that.

Sinclair never changed expression, but the farther down the list he went, the farther the left corner of his mouth turned down. Meanwhile, I was rapidly dressing in a bra, panties, linen walking shorts, a cherry red sweater, and a pair of René Caovilla walking sandals.

"You look like a gladiator in those," was his only comment as he handed my list back.

"I *am* a gladiator. Now let's go!"

"Must we take the subway?" he whined. "We have a private car at our disposal, thanks to Jessica's finely honed sense of guilt."

"It's all part of the definitive New York experience," I said, "so yes."

"So is getting mugged," he muttered, courteously holding the door open for me.

"Don't tease. Wouldn't that be awesome? Something cool to tell my mom."

"Awesome," he replied tonelessly, and followed me out.

Chapter 9

"Wow! It's a good thing I'm dead, or I'd be *exhausted.*"

"As opposed to simply bored out of your charming little mind."

"Oh, shut up. How could we not go up in the building King Kong climbed with Naomi Watts?"

"But darling, he didn't *actually* climb—"

"Stop it, you're ruining the whole thing!"

"The remake, the original, or the evening?"

"You're so talented, you're wrecking all three. Now, what's next?"

"Thankfully, we have completed your interminable list of chores—"

"Five things!"

"—and can now return to the hotel where we will be insulted and threatened by Detective Berry."

We walked on in silence for a moment while I thought about that.

"You can't really blame him for being scared, can you?" I asked quietly.

There was another long pause, and finally Sinclair forced out a reluctant, "No."

"We essentially raped his brain, you know."

No comment from the king of the vampires.

"Just sayin'."

Still no comment. I decided to drop the subject. For the time being.

We were walking hand in hand down Broadway and I *still* couldn't get over the noise. It sounded like noon, and it was nearly midnight! But on the flip side, the cool thing about NYC is that everything was open, practically all the time. We'd had no trouble knocking off my list, even though back in Minnesota, everything would have been closed by nine at the latest. Seven, in winter.

"Spare change?" the zillionth homeless guy asked us, and I smiled at him and gave him a dollar. Sinclair disapproved of this, being a self-made man, but what the hell. I was a rich woman now; legally half of his was mine, and I could do what I liked with my one dollar bills.

But—this was weird—I could hear the homeless guy fall into step behind us. Did he want *more*? Because that was just being greedy. It was one thing to be out of work and ask people for money, but to—

I felt something sharp and pointy against the back of my neck.

"Alley, *now*, fuckers!"

"Which one?" I asked, which I thought was a pretty reasonable question, but he just dug the knife in a little more, pissing me off, and nudged me to the right.

"Rings, wallet, purse," he chanted, once we were off busy Broadway. Obviously a professional.

"I can't believe it!" I gasped.

"*I* can," Sinclair said with his usual air of morbid

disdain. "And if he keeps jabbing you with that pin, I'll be forced to make him eat it."

"We're being mugged! We saw the Empire State Building, the Statue of Liberty, the Met, Ellis Island, and the Central Park Zoo, and now we're finishing the day like *real* tourists!"

"I hate zoos."

"What kind of a communist psycho hates zoos?"

"I'll never get the smell of monkey out of my trousers."

"Rings, wallet, purse, *now*, fuckers!"

"I can't wait to tell my mom!"

"About my trousers?"

"Are you people fucking deaf?" Another jab. Sinclair snarled, but so quietly only I could hear him. "This is a robbery and you gotta give me your shit!"

"Oh, I know what this is," I assured him. I whipped around, faster than he could track, and snatched the knife out of his hand. I bent the blade with my thumb until it was useless as a weapon, then handed it back to him. This was really for his own safety, as God knew what Sinclair would have done to him.

He stared at it, then stared at me, then turned

to run. I thrust my ankle between his and he hit the street.

"You know, I haven't had a bite since we got here," I said. "I mean, besides you."

"I was just thinking the same thing."

We fell on him.

Chapter 10

"You've got an alibi," Nick grumped at dinner the next night. It was early—about seven thirty—which was good, because I had places to be, and couldn't suck down my drinks fast enough.

"Besides our word?" Sinclair asked mildly. He'd given up any semblance of politeness and had brought the paper to dinner, which he was carefully reading. Although we'd been talking for ten minutes, this was the first time Sinclair had spoken up.

"Yeah. Coroner placed the kid's time of death between ten and eleven that night—"

"While the four of us were having dinner," I finished.

"Well, duh, Nick," Jessica said kindly. "You must have known it was a fresh crime scene. Betsy and Sinclair didn't have time to ditch us, kill a child, and return to the table to argue over dessert."

"Mmmff," Nick grunted.

"Yes, an intelligent, unbiased professional would have known that," Sinclair said to the paper.

Astonishingly, Nick didn't rise to the bait. A crisis of conscience, maybe?

"Do you think it was someone here at the hotel?" I asked, almost whispering.

Nick sent me a look of sizzling scorn; I almost wanted to duck. "Of course."

"I doubt it," Sinclair replied absently.

"Come on! If it walks like a duck and quacks like a duck and looks like a duck, it's a fucking duck."

"I have no idea what ducks have to do with your crime scene."

Nick leaned forward, his blonde hair flopping into his eyes. He pushed it back impatiently and said, "I mean, right around the corner from a hotel run by vampires, with vampire guests, a kid gets killed—by a vampire—and you're saying it's got nothing to do with this place?"

"I would be surprised. As Betsy said, vampires don't shit where they eat."

"The smart ones, anyway."

"I'd actually agree with her"—he nearly gagged as he said it—"but what if it's a message?"

"You mean like a note? Except left on the body of a kid?" I felt my gorge rise.

"Yeah. A message for the king and queen. They knew you were coming, right?"

"Of course," Sinclair said carefully. He'd actually laid the paper down.

"So, maybe someone in here is trying to impress you. Pay tribute. Whatever."

"They pay tribute with blood oranges, not ritual sacrifice."

"And they oughta know killing a kid is the *last* thing that will impress us," I snapped.

"Will they?" Nick asked quietly. "Your predecessors were pretty bloodthirsty, right? And aren't you having some trouble being taken seriously by the teeming hordes of the undead?"

"I wish you wouldn't put it like that," I grumbled, downing my Cosmo (hey, we were in New York) in a hurry.

"All they know is that there's a new sheriff in town. My bet is that they're trying to impress you or freak you out. Either way, he—or she—or they—killed that kid to get to you two."

"So what do you suggest we do, Detective Berry?"

He ticked our options off on his fingers. "One: leave town. Now. Tonight. Two: interview every vampire in this building. Thr—"

"Pardon me, Your Majesty." We all looked up and saw the bellboy (bellman) who'd tried to help unpack my shoes when we got here. "The rest of the staff has arrived and await your convenience."

"Thank you, O'Neill. I'll meet with them when we've finished here."

"As you wish, Majesty." He bowed in my direction. "My queen." He ignored Jessica and Nick, but Sinclair must have said they were okay, because otherwise he wouldn't have come up to the table in the first place.

And then he trotted off. I was relieved that he hadn't drowned himself or jumped off a high building after I'd snapped at him our first night, though I'd had no idea he was a vampire.

"You dog!" Jessica exclaimed. "That's why you weren't in the room earlier . . . you were out interviewing suspects."

"Of course. I am not unaware of my responsibilities, though it is always refreshing to have someone less than half my age point them out to me."

Score! I thought it, but didn't say it. Nick had the grace to look abashed. Or was it annoyed? Then he went back into jerk mode and said, "I want to be there for the interviews."

"No," Sinclair said coolly.

"Sinclair, you're not a cop. There's stuff you might miss."

My husband laughed politely.

"Maybe you should—" Jessica began tentatively.

Doing an eerie impersonation of Nick, Sinclair started ticking points off his long fingers. "One: he's out of his jurisdiction. Two: even if he wasn't, this is a vampire matter. Three: with his prejudice, he will be more a hindrance than a help, and four: although there is a killer in the city—perhaps more than one—I owe my people protection. Which does *not* include letting a human policeman find out they're undead."

"Besides," I said, "you have to help me do something instead. Now that Sinclair's going to be tied up."

Nick managed to look mollified and pissed at the same time.

Chapter 11

I knew I looked like a dork, twirling around like Maria in *The Sound of Music*, but I couldn't help it. "Oh, it's all sooooo beautiful!" I cried.

"This is a shoe store," Nick informed me.

"This is the Beverly Feldman shoe store," Jessica said. "It's Betsy's Graceland."

I rushed from one gorgeous shoe to the next. Pumps, flats, sandals! Lace, leather, sequins! Ballet flats! I tried to talk but gurgled instead.

Nick picked up a gorgeous pump with white lace

and a brown bow. "This one is called 'Calm.' So maybe you should buy it."

"Oh, I'll buy it. I'll—miss?"

The saleswoman, an attractive brunette in her thirties, glided over to me. Unobtrusive, yet helpful: just the way I liked 'em. "May I help you?"

I whipped out one of my wedding presents . . . a Black American Express card. I hadn't even known they made them in black. Turns out if you spend more than—I forget exactly, but I think it was two hundred grand—if you spend more than that with Amex in a year, you get a black card. Sinclair had given me mine the day after we got married.

The saleswoman smiled at it.

"I'd like to see Calm, Dabble, Mystery, Ravish2, Splendid, Adore, Amazing, Angelic, Heaven, Infinite, Neat, Phantom, Goblin, Fairy, and Rosella. Oh, and will you deliver these to my hotel?"

"Of course."

"You can't remember to buy milk," Jessica said, "but you memorized most of the Fall Feldman line?"

"Do not ruin this for me. Do *not*."

Once the saleswoman disappeared, Nick took out

his gun. I wasn't sure if he was going to shoot me or himself, and frankly, I had other things to worry about. Luckily, he put it away when she came back, staggering under the load of shoe boxes.

I actually clapped my hands like a kid when I saw her.

Chapter 12

That bastard," Nick fumed in the cab on the way back to the hotel. "He *knew* what he was getting out of. And he knew what you were sticking me with."

"Oh, come on, it wasn't so bad."

"Six hours of shoe shopping!"

"It was only two."

"Well, it felt like a thousand."

"Hey, you wanted to come along on this trip."

"Yeah, well, I was expecting treachery and betrayal and felony assault. *Not* this!"

"Knock it off, you two," Jessica ordered, massaging her temples. "I've got a splitting headache."

In a nanosecond, Nick became a totally different person.

"Babe? You okay? Maybe we better get you back so you can lie down."

"I'm fine, Nick, it's not the cancer. I just have a headache."

Nick was in the middle; I was on his left, and Jessica was on his right. If she hadn't been so thin, it never would have worked. But it did work, which is why I opened my purse, rummaged, then handed Nick a bottle of Advil. He shot me a look of pure gratitude—I almost fell out of the cab—and shook two into his palm, then gave them to Jess, who dry-swallowed them.

"Thanks for coming along, you guys."

"Wouldn't have missed it," Jessica said, leaning back and closing her eyes.

"She's only speaking for herself," Nick added.

"I still can't decide which pair is my favorite," I said dreamily. "Infinite, or Fairy."

"How about Goblin?" Nick muttered. "You just—hey, you're going past our hotel!"

"Sorry, mahn," the driver said calmly. "Got to admit, tough to see dis place on de street."

He had *that* right. The Grange *really* blended, which was weird, given how scary and old-fashioned it looked.

"That's okay," Nick said. "Just take a left and drop us off around the corner."

"Not at all, mahn. I will get you dere." I could see his dark eyes in the rearview mirror, heard him pop the car into reverse, and then we were speeding backward.

"This is a one-way street!" Nick practically shrieked.

"Dis is New York, mahn."

We came to a shuddering halt right outside the lobby steps, and Nick and Jessica couldn't scramble out fast enough.

I handed the driver my last fifty and said, "You got some plums on you, big guy. Keep the change."

He touched two fingers to an imaginary hat and grinned, his teeth very white in his dark face. "Anyt'ing for a pretty lady."

I got out and watched him drive away.

Now *that* was cool. Hideously dangerous and illegal, but cool.

"New York, New York, it's a helluva town," I hummed, trotting up the steps to catch up with Nick and Jess.

Chapter 13

I spotted Sinclair waiting for us in the lounge; he'd already ordered me a Cosmo. I ran up to him, easily outpacing Nick and Jessica, and flung my arms around his neck so hard he rocked back in his chair.

He kissed my temple and said into my hair, "Did you have fun shoe shopping?"

"Oh my God, you would *not* believe it!"

He flinched at "God," rallied, then said, "I'll believe it very well when the American Express bill comes."

"Well, I had to replace the one that's stuck in the wall."

"Ah, so you only bought *one* pair," he teased.

Before I could give him a piece of my mind, or throw my drink at him, Nick and Jess were sitting down at our table. We'd all agreed to compare notes at the end of the evening. Interestingly, now that we were off Nick's suspect list (not that I truly thought we'd ever *really* been on it) we were sort of a crime-fighting team.

Maybe he'd hate us again when we all got back home. Maybe he still hated us but was using us to solve a murder, which would be very Nick-like (and cop-like). Or maybe hanging out with us was loosening him up a little. There was absolutely no way to tell.

"You dirty rotten son of a bitch," Nick started. Okay, maybe there was one way to tell. "You *knew* what her little errand was."

Sinclair actually giggled. *Giggled.* "Which did *you* like best, Detective Berry? Calm or Infinite?"

Nick stuck a finger in my husband's face, which was

a good way to get bitten. "If I didn't hate you with every fiber of my being before, I absolutely do now."

"Somehow," he yawned, "I will try to recover from the remorse."

A pretty waitress—short, good figure, gorgeous green eyes, black hair—bounced up to our table. "Good evening, Majesties! May I bring your guests a drink?"

"Hi," I said, sticking out a hand. Startled, she shook it. "I'm Betsy. This is Nick and Jessica. She'll have a Screwdriver, heavy on the vodka, no ice. He'll have a Bud."

Her hand was clammy and almost uncomfortable to touch, but I held onto my smile and she looked weirdly gratified. "Right away, my queen," she said, and flounced off.

"That, uh, wasn't the killer, was it?" Jessica asked.

"I have been unable to locate the killer. Or if I have, I don't know it yet. But that will change." Sinclair looked grim. Well, grimm*er*. "Of that, I can assure you."

"So, no luck tonight?"

"I believe I just said that."

"Told you I should have been there!" Nick said triumphantly.

"Don't gloat, hon, it's unbecoming," Jessica scolded him gently. "Besides, we were needed elsewhere."

He threw up his hands and sank back in his chair. "Shoe shopping!"

"You don't have to say it like you'd say 'snake milking'."

"Given a choice," he began, when the über-efficient waitress (I bet vampire speed came in handy when you were waiting tables) returned with drinks.

"Thanks a lot, uh—" I squinted, but she wasn't wearing a name tag.

"Marcia."

"Thanks, Marcia. Just charge it to our room, okay?"

"Oh, no."

"Uh . . . will you take a traveler's check?"

"I meant, your money is no good here, Majesty." And she—God, this was so embarrassing—she actually *went down on one knee* and bowed her head to me. "You're The One, the foretold queen, and you've rid us of Nostro and Marjorie in two years.

My life is yours." She looked up, green eyes twinkling. "Or, at the very least, I can pay for your drinks."

"Uh . . . that'll be fine, Marcia." I was so rattled I didn't know what to do. Pat her on the head? Wave her away? Invite her to join us?

Luckily, Sinclair *did* know what to do. "Your loyalty is noted and appreciated, Marcia. Now leave us, dear."

Quick as a snake, Marcia was on her feet and away from the table.

Hmm. Maybe *I* should try that.

"Just in time," Jessica commented. "I was about to puke."

"*I* didn't know she was going to do that," I snapped. "It was so incredibly—"

"Vampire hearing," Sinclair said quietly.

"—nice of her that I was speechless," I amended hastily.

Someone waved at our table, and Sinclair stood. "I've received some faxes from St. Paul. If you'll excuse me."

"Don't think I haven't noticed you keep ditching us," I warned him. "You'll pay."

His eyes gleamed, and he kissed my knuckles. "I look forward to it. Our room, half an hour?"

"Maybe," I sniffed, pretending my thighs weren't already tingling.

"Oh, *barf*," Jessica said. "I never thought I'd wish the cancer would come back to distract me, but . . . "

"Don't even joke about that!"

"So, the bloodsuckers are happy because you're the best of a bad lot, eh?" Nick asked.

"And just when I thought you were done being a dick," I grumbled.

"Honey, I haven't even—wait."

"Wait, what?"

But Nick was looking across the lounge, out into the lobby, where a lone girl was wandering around. She was startling looking, with shoulder-length platinum hair and pale skin. And she was dressed in a white nightgown, in bare feet.

"Must be a kid of one of the guests."

"Yeah, but it's a pretty fucking dangerous place for

a *kid* to be wandering around, don't you think?" Nick was already getting up. "Just a sec."

Jessica and I looked at each other. "Are we really going to let the guys have all the fun on this trip?" she asked.

Then we got up and ran after Nick.

Chapter 14

"Hon? Can I talk to you for a sec?"

The little girl—couldn't have been more than ten—whirled at Nick's voice and I saw she had huge blue eyes, eyes the color of the sky. Then she laughed and ran off.

"Wait! I need to talk to you! Where are your folks?"

All three of us ran after her because—shit!—she had run out the lobby door, out of the (relative) safety of the crowded lobby. Her white blond hair streamed after her like a bridal veil and I thought that I had never seen such a beautiful child. *Real* tempting pickings for the asshole bloodsucker who liked to munch kids.

We came out in time to see her disappear around the block, laughing. I cupped my hands around my mouth and yelled, "We're not playing tag, kid! We gotta talk to you!"

No response. I glanced at my human friends. "Later, gators," I said, because I was going to do my Bionic Woman thing in a sec and they had no chance of keeping up.

But even running as fast as I could, by the time I rounded the block, the kid was nowhere to be seen.

I trudged dejectedly back to them. "That's great. Now we get to wait for another Goddamned crime scene."

"If she lives in the hotel, she probably knows a hundred ways to get back in. Like Eloise," Jessica suggested. "I think she'll be okay. She certainly gave us the slip easily enough."

"Good point," I said, cheering up.

"All the same, I think I'll hang out here for a while," Nick said. "Honey, you go up to the room and get some sleep."

"And leave you out here in the dark by yourself?"

"Uh . . . hon, I'm a cop."

"A human cop looking for a kid-killing vampire! Besides, the Advil worked fine. I'm not even tired."

"Well, shit. That means I have to stay out here, too."

Jessica and Nick both looked surprised. "What are you talking about?" she asked.

"Oh, like I'm really going back inside to have nasty sex with Sinclair while you two are walking around trying to prevent vamp-on-kid crime. That'd only make me the biggest jerk in the world."

"Well—" Jessica began sweetly, but Nick cut her off.

"Seriously, Betsy. Go inside. We'll just walk around out here for a little while and if we don't see anything, we'll come in. And if we do see something, we'll call your cell." He put a (gentle!) hand on my arm. "Really, go. It's your honeymoon, right?"

I was completely torn. Do the right thing, and stick with my human, fragile, easily shreddable friends? Or take the olive branch Nick was so plainly offering? The pleading look on Jessica's face made up my mind for me.

"Okay, but call me if you see or hear anything. We can jump out the window and be on the street in about three seconds."

"Just get dressed first!" Jessica hollered at me as I went up the stairs. *Jerk.*

Chapter 15

Too impatient to take the elevator, I bounded up the eight flights, ran down the hallway, and jammed my key card into the slot. The door obligingly beeped, I entered, then shut the door behind me and started taking off my clothes. Sinclair was already in bed, the covers turned invitingly back. His faxes were neatly piled on the desk—hey, at least he didn't bring them to bed. This time.

"You're flushed," he said, surprised. "Did you feed?"

"No, I ran two blocks in about eight seconds. Nick

saw a kid alone in the lobby and we were worried about her."

"Ah. I trust you warned her."

"Actually, we couldn't catch her. Quick little minx. Jessica thinks she lives here and knows all the alleys and warrens, like a little rabbit. And pretty!"

"Pretty?" he asked doubtfully. (Sinclair wasn't a fan of kids, and barely tolerated BabyJon, my ward and half-brother.)

"Oh my God, you've never seen a prettier kid. She's practically got 'bite me' written on her forehead. So after we couldn't find her, Nick and Jess stayed outside, just in case." I hung my shirt on the shoe in the wall, kicked off my pumps, and stepped out of my shorts. I started to wriggle out of my bra when Sinclair held up a hand; I knew what that meant.

So I walked to the bed and let him gently remove my bra and panties, let him pull me down to him. Then I bit him, hard, on the throat and he bucked beneath me in surprise and pleasure. His cool blood trickled into my mouth like dark wine (irony: I hate wine) and my head started to swim almost immediately.

I could feel his dick pressing against my stomach, almost jerking like a live thing, and he was still spasming beneath me, so I broke off and licked his blood from my teeth.

"How about *that*?"

In response he rolled me over, pounced on me, and bit me right on the jugular. Now I was the one writhing in pleasure—there was something about being taken, something that was just as fine as doing the taking—I don't know, I can't really describe it.

Then he plunged into me and I shrieked at the ceiling, shrieked and clawed at his back while he drank and thrust, while he filled me up and I filled him up, and I had time for a scant thought

please God don't let the cell phone ring

what?

and then my orgasm was roaring through me like a freight train, and it was times like that that I wondered why I ever bitched about being a vampire.

Sinclair shuddered above me and broke off, and I licked the bite on his neck.

"Cell phone?" he panted.

"Told . . . Jess and Nick . . . to call if . . . they ran into trouble."

He grinned down at me and I stroked his broad back, where my scratch marks were already healing. "Then it's a very good thing they didn't—"

My cell phone rang.

Chapter 16

"Two blks S, hurry!!!!!!!" Jess had texted, and hurry we did.

Instead of dressing, we grabbed hotel robes. Instead of messing with the stairs, we broke the window and jumped out.

I managed to keep my feet, but felt the shock of the landing all the way up to my hips. Never mind. The blond kid was in trouble—or dead. I just knew it.

We got there in just a few seconds and I nearly

skidded in the blood, which was as awful as it sounds, especially in bare feet.

"Oh *no*!"

"Fuck," Sinclair muttered, which was very unlike him. I was the potty mouth in the Sinclair family. But the situation certainly warranted it.

Except . . . it wasn't her. It was a different girl, slightly older, wearing filthy clothes and with dirty hands. Her skin wasn't quite as dark as Jessica's, and already going dusky with death.

A homeless child? A runaway? Whoever she had been, she'd crossed paths with the wrong man—or woman—and wouldn't ever have to worry about finding a place to stay again.

"Where is everybody?" I asked, kneeling beside the child.

"We're the first ones on scene. I've called 911."

"You guys didn't see anything?"

"We didn't even hear anything," Jessica said, sounding very strained. "We just rounded the corner and there she was."

"Oh, the poor poor thing. Look! I count at least three bite marks, the fucking greedy bastard."

"Five," Sinclair said distantly.

"*We don't have to kill*! We only have to take half a pint or so, God*damn* it!"

"Yes, that's been my experience," Nick said quietly.

I turned on him and snarled, "Yes, fucking A right, Nick, you're alive, aren't you? You're walking around allowed to be a perfect asshole, *aren't you*? But this poor kid—this . . ." I stretched out a trembling hand, wanting to touch her, stroke her face, maybe pull her into my arms. Too late, all too late.

Nick seized my wrist. "Betsy, don't! This is a crime scene. Anything you do—change—won't help the cops and it won't help her. Just—don't, okay?"

"Let go of my wrist," I said tonelessly, and he did.

In the background, sirens.

"There's nothing we can do except incriminate ourselves," Sinclair said quietly. "It's time to go. Nick can handle the cops."

He took my hand to help me up and I yanked it out of his grip.

"And we were busy fucking while this kid was getting bled like a pig," I hissed at him. "Don't touch me."

I walked out of the alley, alone.

Chapter 17

Jessica caught up with me. "You're not mad at them, you know. You're mad at the creature doing this under your nose."

"Go away."

"Oh, you can just shitcan the attitude, Miss Thang! *I* didn't kill her. In fact, you and your boy-toy wouldn't even know about her if I hadn't told you. So spare me the 'tude."

I didn't say anything. What could I say? She was right.

"We'll get him, Betsy. We won't leave New York until he's in flames or bristling with so many stakes he looks like a hedgehog."

I laughed; I couldn't help it. Quite the mental image!

"There now, that's better." She tucked a hand under my elbow. "And can you slow down? We're not all six feet tall, y'know?"

"I know, how do you stand it? Is it like being a bug? Or is it more like, you know, being an inanimate object? With no real clue what it's like to not be a midget?"

"Shut up, Miss Thang," she ordered, but naturally I disobeyed.

"You don't even—hey!" I stopped, which jerked Jessica to a stop. Sitting on the hotel lobby steps was the girl we'd seen earlier. Thank God! "Hey, you! We've been looking for you!"

"Try to sound a little more menacing, why don't you?" Jess muttered.

The gorgeous child pointed at me. "I know you! We were playing tag earlier!"

"Uh, not exactly. Listen, where are your folks? This is so not a place for a little kid to be by herself, okay?"

"I'm *not* a little kid."

"Right, whatever, where are they?"

"They're dead."

Jessica and I traded glances. That explained why the kid was up at practically midnight.

"But what are you doing here?"

"I live here." She had a high, sweet voice. "The staff takes care of me."

"Uh . . . about the staff . . . I've got some news you're not going to like, but you can't stay here another night. Another minute. Y'see—"

"The hotel is run by vampires?"

Jessica and I looked at each other again.

"Well, yes," Jessica answered. "You, um, knew that?"

"Sure." The child idly examined her nails, which were brutally short—probably because she bit them. "Vampires killed my folks, and the staff felt bad, so they took me in."

"But what about school?"

"Tutors."

"What about a proper bedtime?"

"I sleep during the day, like my guardians."

"But–but . . ." There were things wrong with this scenario, right? Then why couldn't I think of any?

"But don't you want a normal life?" Jessica asked. "I bet a looker like you would get adopted in about five seconds."

"And go live in the suburbs and attend public school and do chores for an allowance and fight with siblings?" The child rolled her eyes. "When I'm living in the greatest city in the world, with no bedtime, brilliant tutors, and thirty parents who watch out for me? Not to mention twenty-four-hour room service?"

"You've got us there," I admitted. "What's your name?"

"Bernadette, but everybody calls me Bernie."

"Well, Bernie, I guess I'm one of your guardians now, too. See, I'm the vampire queen."

Bernie blinked, then started to laugh. She actually rolled around on the steps, she was laughing so hard.

"It's not that ludicrous," I mumbled.

"It really kind of is," Jessica whispered back.

"You! Oh! Oh, not you! It's not you! *You're* not the queen!"

I stomped my bare foot and realized anew I was wearing nothing but a hotel robe. "I am, too!"

"What is going on here?" Sinclair said, startling me badly. I'd never heard him come up behind me.

"Hey, it's her!" Nick said happily, coming up on Jessica's left. "And she's okay!"

"Who is 'her'?" Sinclair asked icily. I guess he was still pissed about the tantrum I'd thrown in the alley. Well, I'd make it up to him later.

"This is Bernie, the kid I was telling you about. But she's safe!"

"That," Sinclair said, "is no child."

Bernie abruptly quit laughing. "Now him," she said to me, smiling prettily, "he's the king, yes. I can believe that. They told me you were young, but there is no way in hell *you* killed Nostro and Marjorie. You spent the evening shoe shopping!" She looked at Jessica. "And it's not you, either. You're just a human. So where is she? Where's the *real* queen?"

"Wh-what are you talking about?"

"You're making a fatal mistake, Bernie, and you won't be the first to underestimate The One."

The kid scowled. "Oh, hush up, Vampire King. You don't know what you're talking about."

"Your greed—and your bite marks—gave you away," Sinclair informed the kid. "Too narrow for an adult vampire."

I whirled on him. "You *knew* a kid was doing this?"

"I suspected. The second victim confirmed it. Really, Bernie. *Five* bites? It's a wonder you haven't been caught before."

"The staff," Jessica rasped, then cleared her throat. "The staff protects her."

Bernie stood, so quickly it was like she teleported to her feet. "The staff fears me," she said, "as should you. Now get out of my hotel."

And with that, she turned and bounded up the steps into the Grange Hotel.

We all stared at each other, and then I broke the silence with an unoriginal, but heartfelt, "Get that little bitch!"

And up the steps we went.

Chapter 18

We chased her through the lobby and across the lounge, around tables like a crazy game of tag. Which I'm betting Bernie thought this was. The staff and guests stared at us, or ignored us—I guess the true (human) New Yorkers were the ones who were ignoring us.

"Help me!" Bernie shrieked as we closed the distance (we had adult legs, after all). "They're going to kill me!"

I didn't dare look back to see if anyone was coming

to the rescue; Bernie had proved before that she could disappear like a rabbit in a hat. I had no intention of taking my gaze off her.

Then, in a case of truly awful timing, the elevator dinged, the doors slid open, and a family of four stepped out. *Who the hell goes sightseeing at midnight?* Quick as thought, Bernie snatched the toddler right out of his stroller, holding him up by his neck. The parents didn't even have time to scream before the doors slid closed and she was gone.

"Text me!" I yelled as Sinclair shoved the stairwell door open and started pounding up the stairs. I followed him, fishing out my phone.

"888888888888888888888!" Jess texted.

"That's our floor," I muttered. What with the window fixers and the crazy vampires, it was gonna get mighty crowded up there. "What the—eighth floor!" I called up to my husband, who was already a flight ahead of me. I heard the door slam open again and knew Nick was doing his best to back us up, though he was four floors away.

In a few more seconds, we were in our hallway and Bernie was holding the squalling toddler and kicking at our door. "Let me *in*, you idiot!" she was screaming, while the kid wailed and wriggled.

Sinclair wrenched a lamp fixture off the wall and flung it straight at Bernie's head. It landed dead on; she shrieked, clutched her head, and forgot all about the kid, who she dropped.

I ran as fast as I could, slid on my knees the last couple of feet (argh, rug burn!), and *just* caught him before he hit the carpet. I knew the room next to us was unoccupied—at least, I'd never heard anyone in there the entire time we'd been at the Grange—so I bounded to my feet, kicked that door open, tossed the kid into the middle of the king sized bed, and shut the door with one hand while texting Jess, "Kid in 810 SAFE!"

I emerged just in time to get knocked sprawling as Bernie and Sinclair fought. She was on him like a cat, clawing and biting and shrieking, and he was slamming his back against the wall, trying to shake her loose.

"Oh no you *don't*!" I yelled, and seized two handfuls of her gorgeous hair. Then I yanked. Hard.

She yowled (I just couldn't get the cat metaphors out of my head) and twisted with frightening speed and agility, and then her little hands were around my throat and I jerked my head back just in time to avoid her slashing fangs. God, she was fast! Those kids never had a chance. Frankly, the outcome of this fight was in doubt, and I was three feet taller.

I wrenched her hands off and threw her—hard—into the wall. Plaster cracked and dust fell everywhere. Nobody was breathing, so nobody cared.

She sprang at me again, and again I batted her away like a fly—barely. And still she came at me, so this time I hit her with a closed fist. I could feel the bones in her face break, and still she wouldn't quit.

Meanwhile, I could hear Sinclair frantically searching rooms—I was betting for a wooden chair leg.

"Bernie, just *stop*!" Wincing—I couldn't believe I was beating up a child—I hit her again. This time her nose broke, and black blood trickled down to her lips.

"I can't! You have to kill me. Why would I stop?"

Because I can't bear to hurt you. Because even though you're a monster, you look like an angel. Because somebody, a long time ago, really *hurt you, and I want to make that up to you.*

One of her little fists got past me and all of a sudden there was a ringing in my left ear. I shook it off and heard the stairwell door open, heard Nick run past us to the room where the toddler was still crying. Thank God. Thank God.

I caught her next fist in mid fly and broke her wrist. She screamed and tried to kick me. So I did what any asshole would do; I let go of her wrist, grabbed her by the ears, and twisted.

She fell to the carpet, all the fight out of her. But the awful thing was, she was looking up at me and trying to smile. Looking up at me, with her head twisted halfway around. I'd broken her neck, but she was still alive.

"I guess . . . I guess you really are the queen."

I dropped to my knees beside her. "Bernie, I'm so sorry. I-I-It wouldn't have been my choice to kill you. If only you weren't so fucking bloodthirsty!"

"It's all right," she said faintly. "It was bound to happen eventually. I just didn't think a blond fashionista would do it."

"Well, uh, thank you."

"I lied."

"Which time?"

She reached for me and, wary of a trick, I took her hand. But she only squeezed it and said, "The staff—it's not their fault. I'm small, but I'm old. I was made when they were building the Brooklyn Bridge. No one else here is more than forty, and they're afraid. It's why they didn't help—didn't help the others. Don't—punish them."

"I won't." Maybe. "But who did this to you, Bernie?"

"You idiot, is your attention span so limited? You did!"

"I meant, who made you into a vampire?"

"Oh." Bernie managed a nod—it was a gruesome sight—over my shoulder. I looked—and saw Sinclair standing there with a snapped-off chair leg.

"No!" I almost screamed. "No, no, no, it's not true!"

Then Sinclair ducked, and the redheaded bellboy (bellman) went sailing over his shoulder.

"Robert," Bernie said faintly. "At last."

I nearly swooned onto the carpet. "Ha! I knew Sinclair hadn't killed you. And what were you doing in our room?"

"Snooping," he admitted.

Robert slowly got to his feet, pale even for a vampire. "Oh, Bernadette, what did they *do*?" He glared at me. "You'll die screaming, you pretender! You—"

"You did all this? You killed her parents, killed *her*? Made her into this–this thing that eats kids? And then took your time coming to the rescue, you fucking coward? She was kicking our door and screaming for help and you only came out *now*?"

"I can hear you, you know," Bernie murmured. "And of course he's a coward. He preys on children. Of course," she added thoughtfully, "so do I. But that's more a size issue for me."

Robert rushed at me (I guess he wasn't interested in answering any of my questions), and I was bracing myself for the attack when there were three quick shots and his head exploded. Just when I thought the week couldn't get yuckier.

He fell, barely two feet from Bernadette's body, and then I saw Nick, who had the toddler on one hip and his gun in his right hand.

Sinclair snapped the chair leg in half (luckily, it was a nice, long slender one) and plunged a piece into Robert's back, all the way through him and into the carpet.

Then he handed the other piece to me.

"I can't," I cried.

"You'd better," Bernie wheezed. "I'll look ridiculous walking around like this. And as for catching prey? No chance."

I raised the chair leg. "I'm sorry, Bernie. And I forgive you for the others."

"I'm not at all sorry and you're a fool to forgive. Good-bye, Vampire Queen."

I shoved the stake all the way in and the light went out of those beautiful blue eyes. Her hand tightened on mine, then went limp.

I pulled her into my embrace, shuddering at the way her head lolled and rolled, and rocked her back and forth, crying. "I'm sorry I'm sorry I'm sorry I'm sorry I'm—"

The elevator dinged and then Jessica was kneeling beside me. "Oh, Betsy. You had to."

"—sorry I'm sorry I'm sorry I'm sorry—"

"Elizabeth, we must—"

"Is everybody okay? I gotta get this kid back to his parents."

"—I'm sorry I'm sorry I'm sorry—"

"Elizabeth—please—"

"I think she's in shock," Nick worried. "Can vampires go into shock?"

In the end, it took all three of them to wrench her out of my arms and I think—I think I fainted or something, because I don't remember much after that.

Chapter 19

I opened my eyes to a familiar sight . . . a ring of concerned faces hovering over me.

"Sorry," I said faintly. I covered my eyes. "That was—that was bad there. For a minute."

"It was fairly awful for all of us, so don't beat yourself up," Jessica assured me. "We're just glad you and Sinclair are all right."

Silence. Then I heard Jess stomp on Nick's foot, and his stifled yelp. "Aren't *we*?"

"Yeah, yeah."

"Thanks for killing the bellman," I said. "That must have felt good."

"I only shot him in the head. I have no idea if that kills you guys. I think Sinclair delivered the coup de grace, as it were."

"But he was coming after me. He was coming after me, and you shot him three times in the head."

"Yeah, yeah."

I smiled for the first time in what felt like weeks.

"My poor Elizabeth," Sinclair said, sitting down beside me on the bed. He picked up my hand—my killing hand, my stake-wielding hand—and kissed it. "You won't be naïve much longer at this rate. Pity."

"Right now I feel about a thousand years old."

"Well, you look great," Jessica assured me. "Your hair isn't even messed up."

That cheered me up a little. "So what happens now?"

"The staff helps us cover this up, of course. They're walking around on eggshells right now, wondering what we'll do to them."

"I promised Bernie we'd leave them alone."

"That doesn't mean," Sinclair said grimly, "that we can't stop in now and again and check on them."

"You mean, like a second honeymoon?" Jessica teased.

I groaned. "Jesus Christ, let me recover from this one first!"

As jokes went, it was fairly lame, but we were all so stressed out we laughed anyway. And then it was better.

I was just glad I didn't have nightmares since coming back from the dead, because I knew Bernie'd be haunting my thoughts plenty when I was awake.

But that was a worry for another time; right now I had to focus on getting rid of Jess and Nick, and finishing my honeymoon without worrying about dead children popping up and ruining the mood.

And that's exactly what I did.

Survivors

The Whiskers are trying to survive in a hostile new area after being evicted from their manor by the vicious Commandos.

—*Meerkat Manor*,
Animal Planet

★

SURVIVOR: noun. 1) One who lives through affliction. 2) One who outlives another. 3) An animal that survives in spite of adversity.

★

Just sit right back and you'll hear a tale,
A tale of a fateful trip
That started from this tropic port
Aboard this tiny ship.

—"The Ballad of Gilligan's Island,"
by George Wyle and Sherwood Schwartz

For my children,
who got me hooked on Animal Planet.
Now you'll all have to suffer for it.

Author's Note

The events of this novella take place after *Swimming Without a Net*, the second Fred the Mermaid book.

Chapter 1

This is Con 'Bad Baby' Conlinson. I'm just like you . . . only I'm on TV. I've gotten really close to the summit of Everest, spent the night in the Everglades (Motel™), faced down numerous angry dogs and cats, gotten thrown out of no less than seven—*seven*—bars, surfed the insanity of Lake Ontario, stayed dry in Seattle, and been audited twice.

"I've been through it all, and I'll show you how to

survive all that and worse in . . . *Con Con the Survivin' Man* (pronounced 'mahn,' or so I keep reminding my producer). Tonight's episode, Con Conlinson *stupidly tells the crew to take their boat and separate, resulting in THE GIANT FUCKING MESS I find myself in this evening.*"

Newly stranded, Animal World™'s Conwin Edmund Conlinson sighed and stared at the sky. The glorified rowboat rocked and swayed in this, a more or less unoccupied stretch of the Pacific Ocean.

And it hadn't seemed like that much of a storm, either.

Con sighed again. When he stretched out, the boat was a foot longer than his head and his feet. The craft itself was little more than a couple of life jackets, a tarp, a first aid kit (which he hadn't needed; he'd come through the storm without a scratch . . . or a *crew*), a knife, a flint, a notebook that he took to be some sort of log, and a box of blue Bics.

No food, of course. Or fishing gear.

Or land.

Just that silver coconut that had managed to keep

a perfect distance between him and his boat for the last several hours, no matter where he drifted. He watched it bob, bored. He supposed he could start a diary. But he was a TV guy, not a journalist. TV guys weren't known for their writing skills. But give 'em a teleprompter and they went to town! Yeah!

And what would he write about, anyway? How, in his arrogance, he'd wanted a smash-bang season opener of *Con Con the Survivin' Man* (mahn), how he'd insisted on keeping distance between his little boat and the larger rig, the one with the camera crew, the producer, and the *food*.

How he'd ignored the storm, instead shouting survival tips to the camera over one shoulder while braving the squall. How he'd lost his balance and gone sprawling, how everything had gone starry and dark, and by the time he sat up, the crew boat was nowhere in sight. The storm had howled and *nothing* was in sight, and for a while he'd assumed he was in real trouble. And all this before sweeps week!

But just as suddenly as it had sprung up, the storm disappeared, leaving him stranded.

Yeah, he'd write *all* about that. He could see it now: *The Memoirs of Captain Dumbass. Chapter One: I forget every single nautical rule of safety and survival.*

No, he was in a mess of his own making, and writing about it wasn't going to help. He and the silver coconut were on their own.

And where did *that* come from?

Well. It was the only thing to look at, for one thing; small wonder most of his attention was fixed on it. Wherever he looked he saw the endless ocean, the cruel unrelenting sea (hey, that was poetic, kinda, he should remember it for his triumphant comeback show), no islands, no greenery, no birds . . . just the silver coconut.

The survival expert flopped back into the bottom of the boat and realized that he had never seen a silver coconut. And the nearest tree was probably a zillion nautical miles from here. He studied the sky, which was an irritatingly cheerful blue. A "no dumbass got his bad self abandoned on my watch" kind of blue. The most annoying blue in the world, come to think of it. *Arrggh.*

He sat up, scowling. Better to look at the coconut. Which was quite a bit closer. Maybe the tides had changed? No, that didn't make any sense. Maybe—

The coconut had a face. The coconut was a severed head!

Chapter 2

"Oh Gawwwwwwd help me!" he cried in a baritone that would have sent gulls screaming from their perches—if there had been any gulls. He flopped back down in the boat.

Just what he needed. Tom Hanks's character in *Cast Away* had Wilson the volleyball; he, Con Conlinson, would have Silver Severed Head. He should have listened to his mother. She'd wanted him to take the Civil Service exam and stay the hell out of showbiz.

He peeked over the rim of the boat. The head was

very close now. He could see at once why he'd mistaken it for a silver coconut . . . the face was very pale, the eyes wide open, with silver pupils and long, flowing silver hair. Not old lady silver. *Silver* silver. The color of old nickels, polished by an obsessive. It was sort of striking and frightening at the same time.

The cold, dead lips opened. The silver eyes blinked. "Do you require assistance, biped?"

He flopped back down in the boat. Day two, and already the hallucinations were setting in. No fresh water, no food. What had he been thinking, taking the smaller, poorly equipped boat? He hadn't, that was all. After all, the crew was always there to pull him out of a jam. Why should last weekend be any different?

"Excuse me?" the severed head said, *much* closer. "Are you all right?"

He flopped an arm over the edge and heaved himself off the bottom of the boat, making it rock alarmingly. The severed head was *very* close now, only a few feet away. And . . .

"Holy shit, a mermaid!"

"If you like. I am of the Undersea Folk. And you have not answered my question."

"A friggin' mermaid, right here next to me! I thought you were a severed head!"

The mermaid swam cautiously closer, easily parting the water with her long, pale arms. Her silver hair streamed behind her. She was sleek and pale and sweetly plump; her round face was set in a frown. "I think you have been exposed overlong to the sun."

He stuck his hand over the side of the boat. She stared at it. "I'm Con Conlinson. Well. Just Con."

Tentatively, she reached up and brushed his fingers with her cool, wet ones. "I am Reanesta."

He burst out laughing. Maybe he *had* been in the sun too long. "Seriously? That's your name? Reanesta? It sounds like a prescription sleeping pill."

"I do not know what that is. And you have not answered my question, which, in a way, answers my question."

"Huh?"

She disappeared with a flip of her silver tail and reappeared seconds later on the other side of the boat. She shook her head so that her long hair fell back, and blinked water out of her eyes. "Your craft is intact," she announced, startling him so that he nearly fell overboard. "And you have the means to propel yourself elsewhere." She gestured to the oar. "So are you harmed? Or ill?"

"No, I'm fine." Also: dazzled, besotted, horny. Those eyes. That hair. Those—

"Then why are you still here?"

"Where am I gonna go?"

She seemed taken aback and made a vague gesture, one encompassing the ocean. "Where would you *not* go?"

"Uh . . . I don't have a tail. Not that I have anything against tails. Particularly yours. In fact, yours is gorgeous," he hastened to assure her.

"Gorgeous?" she repeated doubtfully.

"Gorgeous." It was the color of candlefish, all sleek silver, wider at the hips and narrowing to wavy silver fins. "In fact, you are *really* gorgeous." And those tits! He was having a terrible time maintaining eye contact. She was delectably curvy, and her breasts bobbed sweetly in the water, the nipples so pale a pink they were almost cream colored. She was like a ghost . . . or a dream.

"No, I am ugly," she replied simply, as if she were

explaining that two and two made four. "And I think you must be ill. Perhaps you should rest. Or eat."

"Ugly!" He nearly toppled out of the boat again. "Are you shitting me?"

"I . . . do not believe so."

"You've at least got some meat on your bones, unlike all those anorexic big-mouthed Hollywood brats. Your hair—your tail—your eyes—your ti—your brea—you're the best-looking woman I've ever seen. Ugly! Sheee-it!"

"Well," she said, swimming idly around the boat, "my blubber does keep me warm."

"We're in the South Pacific," he said, feeling stupid. "What do you need to keep warm for?"

"I travel all over. And if you swim to the bottom, it can be chilly. But my coloring is bad. My friends are yellow and blue and green and anything you can imagine. I am"—she looked down at herself—"I'm a noncolor. I am practically not here."

"Noncolor, my Alabama butt."

"Your—what?"

"Where I come from, silver's just about the most

precious thing there is. We use it for money. It's *really* valuable. And pretty."

"The habits of bipeds are not known to me," she admitted, rolling over on her back. She idly splashed with her tail, and yawned. "That is why I followed you for the last two days. When you seemed, ah, confused, I thought I might offer assistance."

"Well, that was nice of you." *Two days?* "Appreciate that."

"Due to recent events among my people, we are allowed to show ourselves now."

"Get outta here!"

"I beg your pardon." She splashed, harder, and he was instantly drenched from eyebrows to belt buckle.

He coughed for five minutes while she watched impassively and finally wheezed, "Sorry, it's a biped saying meaning to express shock or amazement. I remember, I saw it on CNN! You guys have been in hiding for, what, centuries?"

"Indeed. But our great king, in his wisdom, has decreed that if we wish to show ourselves to surface dwellers, we may. But you are the first one I've seen so close."

"Well, I'm honored."

She seemed oddly pleased. "Thank you."

"So, you live around here?"

"I live all over."

"Ever been on land?"

"Yes."

"Ever been to an Alabama barbeque?"

"No."

"That was a joke."

She frowned. "It wasn't funny."

"Well, I'm tired. And thirsty. And starving. Shouldn't have mentioned barbeque. I— hey, where'd you go?" Because she'd disappeared, dropping out of sight with a flash of her tail.

"Well, sheee-it," he muttered. "Meet the prettiest gal ever and scare her away in five minutes. Nice work, Con."

It didn't seem to be his week, that was for damned sure.

Chapter 3

A couple of minutes later, she was back.

"Say, hi there!"

"Hello again." She tossed shiny things into his boat. Tiny . . . headless things. Fish. She had caught and killed three small silver fish for him.

"I am aware that bipeds can be unusually squeamish," she said, picking a scale out of her unusually sharp teeth, "so I killed them for you."

His gorge rose, and he fought it down. This wasn't a meal, this was bait! "Uh, thanks, Ree."

"Reanesta."

"Yeah, I'm stickin' with Ree. I, uh, it's not that I'm not grateful, but I can't eat these like this."

"Like what? Shall I bite the fins off for you?"

"No!" he shouted. Then, more quietly, "I mean, no thank you. Listen, I couldn't never even eat sushi without wanting to puke."

She frowned at him. "But you need the moisture as well as the protein."

"I *know*. But I can't. It's a mental block thing."

"You require them cooked?"

"Yup."

"But we have no fire. So you must eat them as they are."

"Yeah, but I can't." Inwardly: *Some survival expert!* Well, what his viewers didn't know wouldn't hurt them. "See, usually my crew has food, and I don't have to actually *do* the things I tell people to do."

"Watch me, Con. It's easy." And she reached into the boat, snatched up a fish, and crunched. He watched, wide-eyed, as she demolished the thing with her small, sharp teeth, wiping a dot of blood off her cheek when she was finished. "Ah! Delicious. See?"

He leaned over the boat and retched. *Oh, you're making a great impression, asshole!* he thought as he barfed.

"Oh, dear."

"Please don't do that again," he begged.

"I foresee problems ahead."

"Ya think?"

"Let me do so," she said. "I will come back." And she was gone again.

He lay back in the boat and thought about what an idiot he was.

Chapter 4

He must have dozed, because a gentle rapping on the lone oar woke him up. He sat up and there was Ree, holding out a fistful of what looked like puffy seaweed.

"We call this Traveler's Grass," she explained. "It grows in salt water, but it won't dehydrate you and will fill your stomach."

"Well, I never was a salad man, but you know what they say about beggars and choosers."

"No."

"Never mind," he said, accepting the clump of seaweed. He put some cautiously in his mouth, chewed, then took another bite.

"Slowly," she cautioned, "or you will vomit again."

"Don't wanna do *that*," he said with his mouth full. This . . . wasn't bad. A little briny, sure, but his stomach wasn't resisting and that was the important thing. And the more he ate, the more he wanted. He finished the fistful in less than a minute. "Wow, thanks, Ree! God, I feel better."

"I will bring you more. I will come back."

"Not one for long good-byes, are you?" he shouted at her disappearing tail.

In another minute she'd brought an armful and plopped it into the boat. "Perhaps once you've had more of this, you'll be sensible about the fish. You must have fresh water."

"For such a pretty gal," he said, chewing, "you're a pretty big nag."

"And for such a helpless biped, you're remarkably unwilling to save your own life."

"Hey, I bet you'll find people all over the world who don't eat raw fish."

"Stupid people. Dead people."

"Aw, go bite the head off another fish."

"Perhaps I will!"

"Well, who's stopping you?" he yelled, still chewing.

"No one at all," she snapped back, and vanished again.

Which was fine with him.

Er, right?

Chapter 5

Reanesta guiltily swam back an hour later. Yes, he had annoyed her with his helpless ways and silly prejudices, but he was sick and, even if he wouldn't admit it, already dying. She had been wrong to take offense and leave.

So she swam up to the boat, which had drifted but not so far she couldn't find it, and politely knocked on the oar again.

His stubbled face popped over the side and he smiled when he saw her, showing those odd, flat teeth common to bipeds. Maybe *that's* why he couldn't eat the fish. It was a wonder they managed to eat anything with those dull things.

"Ree! You came back!"

"Yes. I apologize for arguing. You're ill and unaware of your irrationality."

"Uh . . . thanks, I think." He was looking down at her with those dark eyes, his cheekbones prominent and the stubble on his cheeks an interesting reddish brown. His hair was as dark as his eyes. Like her, he had very ordinary coloring, but she found him interesting all the same.

He was the first biped she'd had the courage to approach. And, she had to admit, she liked that he liked her. Perhaps that was part of his appeal.

"Here." She handed up a fistful of Lallyflowers, the ones that grew in shallower waters, which she was fairly certain he could eat. "Try these."

"Thanks," he said gratefully, and chomped into the yellow petals without hesitation. "And thanks for coming back."

"I was wrong to leave."

"Naw, I was being a jerk."

Privately she agreed, but said nothing.

"These aren't too bad, though if I get out of this I'm never eating a salad again."

"Do you think," she said tentatively, "now that you have something in your stomach, you might try a fish?"

He looked guilty and said around a mouthful of petals, "I chucked 'em after you left."

She inwardly cringed at the waste. No wonder the planet was such a mess! Perhaps her folk should take it away from the bipeds. "If I brought you more?"

He hesitated, then said, "Yeah, okay, I'll give 'er a try. Can't promise to keep 'em down, though."

"Excellent! All right, I will get some. You stay here."

"I wasn't planning on going nowhere," he said dryly, and she flushed, embarrassed—what a stupid thing to say!

"I will come back," she promised, which was something she had never said to anyone in her forty-five years, but which she had said many times to this man. It was very strange.

"I'll be waitin'."

She vanished into the water, darting for the bottom, looking for something he might try to bite. She ignored the manta rays—too big—and the barracudas (same reason), although she knew for a fact both were delicious. She finally settled on a wrasse and two small parrot fish, snatching them and biting their heads off before they could evade her. Then she arrowed back up to the boat, watching as the silhouette got bigger and bigger until she popped out of the water.

"Oh, great, you're back," he said with a marked lack of enthusiasm.

"You said you'd try," she scolded him gently. She handed him one of the parrot fish.

He sniffed it, shuddered, and nibbled on one of the fins.

"No, no. You have to *bite*. You'll never get any protein that way. I know! Hold it over your mouth and squeeze and at least drink the blood."

"You're being," he said, "the opposite of helpful."

"Oh, for the king's—" She seized the side of

the boat, switched to her legs, and heaved herself into it.

He *stared* at her. "Silver hair, uh, all over, I see."

"Yes, yes. Like this." She grabbed the fish and leaned toward him, holding it over his mouth. He was still staring at her. "Open your *mouth*," she said, trying not to lose her temper, and, obediently, he did. She squeezed, and blood trickled into his mouth, over his silly flat teeth and down his throat. She squeezed the fish dry, then dropped it on the bottom of the boat. "Oh, hooray! You did it! Oh, well done!" She bounced and clapped, but quit when the boat started to rock.

"Huh? Did what? Bleeeccchh! What the *hell* did you do?" He spit over the side.

"You drank the whole fish!"

"I did *what*? No fair!" he accused. "You distracted me with your nudity."

"And a good thing, too," she said primly, folding her arms across her chest and crossing her legs. "Otherwise you'd be dead of dehydration. Now. Ready to try another one?"

"Another what?" he said absently, but opened his mouth again, and drank both fish, and afterward they had a terrific argument about the diabolical use of her feminine wiles—whatever that meant—and she jumped overboard and swam away again.

Chapter 6

An hour later, he was still spitting, but couldn't deny he felt better. But it was pretty damn diabolical of her to use her body like that to distract him into—eecccch!—drinking fish blood.

And it had all started so innocently, too! He'd been minding his own business, working on not staring at her tits, when all of a sudden she had *legs* (and like the song said, she knew how to use them) and was clambering into the rowboat.

She was all flashing pale skin and long hair and

silver eyes. Her lips were moving, but he had no idea what she was saying; he was too busy hoping she wasn't noticing his hard-on.

And the next thing he knew, his mouth had tasted like blood and she was cheering, which made her breasts bounce in a really charming way, but didn't lessen his feeling of being tricked.

So they had another fight, and off she went. And good riddance!

But he wasn't entirely surprised when she came back. It seemed she was doomed to always come back. This time she didn't bother knocking, just popped up out of the water and said, "What are feminine wiles?"

"They're when you grow gorgeous long legs and flop into the boat like a wet dream come true, and I'm so busy trying not to stare at your bush and your legs and your boobs and your eyes that you can pretty much talk me into anything."

"And a 'wet dream'?"

"Forget about it."

"But you feel better now, yes?"

"Yes," he grumped.

"Then I think it is past time you left."

He waved his arms around, trying not to fall out of the boat. "We're in the middle of the South Pacific! And I've only got one oar."

"So jump in," she said with barely concealed impatience.

"I, uh, can't swim."

She blinked and said nothing.

"Okay," he said, "I'm well aware of the irony of a survival expert who gets his ass stranded, can't stand to eat raw fish, loses an oar, and can't swim. I'm *aware*, 'kay? But see, I'm the *star*. I don't have to do those things, I just have to be able to tell people about them."

"I had no idea," she marveled, "that bipeds were so completely helpless."

"You shut up."

"And in fact," she pointed out, "you *do* have to do those things."

"Well, I can't," he grumped, "so stop with the nagging."

"That's all right," she soothed.

"*You're* in a good mood."

"I've never had a pet before."

He had just flopped back down, but now bolted upright in outrage. "I'm not your goddamned pet!"

"You are a creature who would die without my help, who needs constant tending, and who cannot get out of trouble on his own. Is that not a pet?"

He sputtered and fought the urge to seize a handful of her long hair and yank. Dimly, part of him realized that he was overreacting, that he was getting in real trouble and needed to get to land and protein pronto, but most of his brain was consumed with rage.

"I am not your fucking pet!"

"Oh, but you are," she went on with maddening cheer. "Do not fear; have I not taken excellent care of you so far?"

He seized the lone oar, wrenched it out of the oarlock, and smacked her over the head with it.

"Ouch!" she cried, while he stared at the cracked oar. She really *did* have a head like a coconut. "Bad, bad biped!"

"Jeez, I'm sorry, I don't know what . . . came . . . over . . ." Then everything fuzzed out and he collapsed back into the boat.

Chapter 7

Reanesta shook him gently, and he eventually opened his eyes and grinned dizzily at her. "Hey, you've got legs again!"

"It was the quickest way to get into the boat. I think you'd better actually *eat* some fish now, instead of just drinking the bl— the fluids."

"I'll tell you, I could murder a steak right now. Oh, and I'm really, really sorry I hit you. You should whip my ass."

"You are not yourself. I was wrong to tease you about being a pet."

"That was teasing?"

"I am not funny," she informed him.

"No, no, it was hilarious." He forced a giggle. "I just, uh, wasn't tracking very well."

"See here," she said. "I have descaled this fish and broken it into small chunks. Won't you sit up and try some?"

"I don't think I can."

"Please, Con?"

He wasn't sure if it was the "please," or her use of his name, or sheer desperation, but whatever it was, it changed his mind. "Okay," he said, and sat up too fast, and the bow dipped and swayed (more than usual) and the sky spun a crazy blue until things settled down. "Oooooh, boy! What day is it?"

"Thursday."

"Really? You guys keep track of the days of the week?"

"Stop stalling and chew."

He opened his mouth to protest, and she stuffed a slimy, fishy chunk inside. He held his nose and chewed, gagged, chewed more, swallowed, gagged again, held his head over the side of the boat, and threw it up.

"Again," she said impassively, but he was so tired and wrung out, even the sight of her breasts hanging in his face failed to distract him, or even interest him that much.

No question: he was dying. The day he didn't take notice of a terrific rack was the day they'd—

"Again," she said, and stuffed another chunk into his mouth. He held his nose again, chewed, swallowed, gagged . . . and kept it down.

She fed him for about half an hour, occasionally disappearing for more fish, which she beheaded, scaled, and chopped up (with her teeth? He didn't want to think about it) before getting back into the boat. He managed to keep about a dozen pieces down.

"I'm sorry," he groaned, tossing his cookies (his rainbow fish) once again. "This must be so disgusting for you."

"It's fine. You're doing quite well. Fear not, you will be home soon."

"Naw, I won't. But you're sweet to say so. I'm gonna nap now, 'kay?"

Her lips were moving, but he had no idea what she was saying, and then his eyes slipped shut and he knew no more.

Chapter 8

When he woke up, the sun was setting and he felt much better. Ree was swimming aimlessly around his boat, and when he sat up she swam straight over.

"How are you?"

"Better. Almost human and everything! Except for the smell. Whoo! How do you stand it, honey?"

"You cannot help it," she said with typical bluntness. "Listen, I have a plan. Perhaps I could try to find another of my kind and we could get help."

He peered at her. "How come you sound so doubtful?"

"You were correct; we *are* in the middle of nowhere. And my telepathic range is very limited. It might take days to find help and by then you'd—ah—"

"Telepathic—oh, right! I read about that, in *Newsweek* I think. How all you mer-guys are telepaths. That must come in handy."

"Right now," she said grimly, "it seems a fairly useless talent."

"Aw, don't be so hard on yourself. I—what's the matter?"

For she had turned her head and was looking off into the distance, straight (or so it seemed to him) into the setting sun.

"That hammerhead shark is back," she said casually.

He nearly shrieked. "Hammerhead?" Then, "Back?"

"Yes, it occasionally noses around, mostly while you're uncon—asleep. I keep warning it away."

"Oh—the telepathy. You talk to fish, too?"

"Of course. But she's heavy with pup and is not inclined to listen. I—oh, in the king's name," she said, exasperated, and this time he could see the fin arrowing out of the water toward Ree.

"I will come back," she said, and dived to meet it.

"Ree!" he screamed. "Get in the boat with me!" But she couldn't hear him, so he lunged over the side—and sank like a stone.

Chapter 9

Luckily, he'd taken a big breath before hitting the water, and even better, the water was warm, but the salt stung his eyes and for a moment he couldn't see anything.

Then he saw Ree darting to meet the shark, which looked like it had about a zillion teeth. He wished *he* was telepathic; he'd tell her to get the fuck away from it. He wished he'd thought to grab the oar on the way down. He wished he'd taken those swim lessons at the Y.

He clumsily swung his arms in the water and made

about half a foot of forward progress. Meanwhile, Ree had deftly caught the shark—an eight footer!—by the jaws and was holding them open. Then she reared up, let go of the jaws, and grabbed it by the hammer-thing. It snapped, but Ree was too quick and it missed her tail by about four inches.

Then—he wondered if the salt was blinding him, because he was having trouble believing his eyes—still holding onto the hammer, Ree somehow lunged forward—and took a bite out of the shark's back!

The shark tried to rear away from her and she let it, giving it a smack on the fin as it sped away from her, trailing blood. Then she turned and her eyes widened as she saw him.

He managed a wave, still sinking, trying to drown without being too much trouble, and she arrowed toward him, seized him under the armpits, then darted toward the surface. He was amazed; she was swimming, with his bulk, even faster than he had sunk.

They popped to the surface and he took a breath, then coughed. "Lucky I was there to save your ass," he gasped, suddenly conscious of her breasts pressing against the back of his T-shirt.

She heaved him into the boat like a sack of potatoes—Christ, she was strong!—not once letting up with the scolding. "What were you thinking, stupid Con? You cannot swim! You would have had *no* chance against a pregnant shark, particularly that breed. She was starving, which is the only reason I did not kill her, but if she comes back I *will* kill her, and you, too, if you do such a foolish thing ever again."

"Couldn't let you get eaten on my account."

"We are the top of the food chain in the ocean, as you are on land, stupid Con! I was in no danger."

"Now you tell me," he mumbled.

She paddled agitatedly around the boat for a minute, then said, "I cannot put this off any longer. You need land."

"Now you tell me," he said again.

"I do not know how long it will take. It may take too long."

"Whatever," he said, yawning.

She seized the bow (or was it the stern?) of the boat with one hand and started to swim. Slowly, the boat started to move. He tried to sit up, thinking he could help row with the (broken) oar, but saw at once it was no good—he'd cracked it too thoroughly on her head.

So he flopped back in the boat and dozed. He had no idea what she was up to, but felt perfectly safe. Anyone who could fight off a hammerhead in ten seconds could certainly manage *his* destiny.

Chapter 10

He woke up to a gorgeous sunrise, to see Ree stumbling through the surf, dragging the boat behind her. "We are here," she croaked, looking at him with enormous dark-ringed eyes. She staggered forward onto the sand of the small beach and collapsed, deeply asleep almost at once.

He scrambled out of the boat (which she had considerately hauled up on land for him) and went to her, gently touching her shoulder. She must have hauled the boat all fucking night, he thought, appalled and amazed. And was out cold from sheer exhaustion.

He stripped off his shirt and covered her with it, then went to look for firewood. The island was tiny—he could walk the length of it in less than ten minutes—but had lots of shrubbery and trees, and he had no trouble finding plenty of kindling and firewood. Then he went to the rowboat and found the matches.

One thing he *could* do was start a fire with a minimum of matches, and the wood was nice and dry. By the time Ree woke up, he had a nice blaze going.

"Oh, good, now you can cook," she said groggily, sitting up and shaking the sand out of her hair.

"I can't believe you towed the boat all night! You're an angel!"

"Oh, well," she said modestly, but looked pleased. "I am a hungry angel. I will come back."

"Wait!" He pressed her back into the sand. "Aren't you pooped? Maybe you should rest awhile."

"No," she said firmly, removing his hands from her shoulders. "I have responsibilities."

"I'm not your damned pet!"

"Yes, but you have no fishing gear and are still

starving. Also, did you find the fresh stream on the north side of the island?"

"Yes," he admitted. "But there's plenty of coconuts we can eat; they're all over the ground."

"Cooked fish will be better for you." She stood, shaking out her long hair. Then seemed to remember something. "I, ah, apologize for my appearance."

He goggled at her. "Huh?"

"I am aware of your cultural taboo against nudity. If I had clothes I would wear them, so as not to offend you."

"Uh, Ree, where I come from, a gorgeous woman walking around naked is *not* offensive."

She relaxed. "Oh. Perhaps I was misinformed. Very well. I will come back."

"I'll be here," he promised, watching her dart into the surf and make the cleanest dive he'd ever seen. Her legs went in and he saw a saucy flash of her tail and then she was gone. Again.

He flopped back down in the sand. God, it was so great to be on land and out of that nasty little boat! And with fascinating company, no less. If he ever got out of this mess, he'd have the most amazing comeback show in the history of the channel! He'd tell them all about Ree and how she saved his life and fought a shark and tugged the boat to an island and brought him food. And—

Wait.

If he got out of this—if he was rescued—he doubted Ree would come with him. And what would he do without her? He'd *die* without her.

Wait.

Once he was back on land, he wouldn't be in any danger. He wouldn't need Ree.

Except that felt like the biggest lie on land *or* sea.

Chapter 11

Reanesta felt much better once she hit the water. It had been a long, exhausting night and for a while she feared she'd lost her bearings and wouldn't find the island. But her sense of direction had not deserted her, and just as the sun was coming up she spotted it. By then she was so tired her limbs were shaking and she feared she might vomit like Con frequently did.

Instead, she dragged the boat up on shore and immediately went to sleep. When she woke, it was to burning brightness and she realized that her helpless biped could do at least *one* thing. Besides make her feel strange in her stomach.

The strangeness was probably impatience, she thought, snatching two wrasse and three pinfish. He was definitely the most infuriating creature she had ever met. Were all bipeds like that? she wondered. What had Fredrika Bimm gotten them into?

She was still pondering that when she sloshed back up to the beach. She knelt by the fire, trying not to wince away from it, expertly spitted the fish on a long branch, and planted the branch in the sand, occasionally turning it so the fish cooked evenly.

Con came loping out of the darkness, and already looked much improved. The fresh water, she decided, and now he smelled like coconuts, so his stomach was full. That was good. Of course, just about anything would have been an improvement.

"Any problems? Look who I'm asking!" he cried, answering his own question. "Like there's anything you can't handle. You should have the survival show."

"Mmmm," she said, turning the fish again.

"God, that smell is driving me *crazy*," he said,

flopping down on the sand. "I—are you okay? Your eyes are all squinty. It's the fire, isn't it? It's bothering you?"

"A little. They aren't common at the bottom of the sea," she said, trying another joke.

"Well, ooch over, I'll cook."

"Uh—"

"I'm not *that* helpless," he said, exasperated. He nudged her in the ribs and she obediently moved over a foot. Instantly her eyes felt better. "You think they're done yet? They're done, aren't they?"

"Not quite."

"I got a dumb question, here."

"I," she teased, "am not surprised."

He smacked her on the thigh and she laughed. "How do you know how to cook on land?"

"We have banquets—great parties and celebrations—on land. And there is much cooked food at these feasts. The prince in particular enjoys cooked food, so we all learn how to make it when we're still pups."

"Pups? Baby mermaids?"

"Yes."

"What's the prince like?"

"Infatuated," she said shortly, picking up a stick and drawing her name in her own language, a complicated grouping of loops and swirls incomprehensible to anyone but her own kind.

"Oh, yeah? You jealous?"

She snorted. "Hardly. I have only met him twice. I do not know him well enough to be jealous of his love affairs."

"Affairs, plural?"

"But because he fell in love with the half-breed—I mean, Fredrika—" She blushed at her rudeness. After all, she had been at the Pelagic, hadn't she? And Fredrika had handled herself quite well under the circumstances. She had a startling manner about her, a grimness cloaked in sarcasm, but still—she had acquitted herself well at the Pelagic, well enough that—

"Ree? Hello? Come back, Ree." He was snapping his fingers before her face in an extremely irritating matter. "Fell in love with the gal who basically talked the king into letting you guys come out of the closet," he prompted. "Read it in *People*."

"Well. Yes. She has a great deal of influence with the royal family and I—I am not sure that is the best thing for my people. After all, she spent nearly all of her years on land, being raised by your kind. She knows nothing of Undersea Folks. And," she added in a mutter, "she comes from bad blood."

"Oh, yeah? What's that mean? My daddy was a trucker."

"Her 'daddy' was a traitor. But the prince—and the king—turn a blind eye to this, and, as I said, she has great influence with the royal family."

"Well, it's a goddamned good thing she does, otherwise I'd be dead of dehydration by now."

"Now that is a good point," she said, cheering up. "I never would have dared approach you even six months ago."

"Months? You have calendars?"

"Don't be absurd. The fish are done." She yanked the stick out of the sand, popped a fish off, and tossed it to him. He tore into it, ingesting a good deal of scales along with the cooked meat, but there were no complaints this time. He wolfed down the second, as well.

"Don't you want the last one?"

"I ate while I was hunting."

"Oh, good." He sucked down most of the last fish, then let out a small, contented burp. "Oh, man, that is so much better."

"You look better," she informed him. "Of course, you could hardly look worse." He smelled better as well; she assumed he had splashed about in the surf and cleaned up a bit. He was shirtless, but still had those—what were they called?—blue jeans?—on.

"Thanks for that. And for the fish. Delicious."

"They're just fine raw," she muttered. "Stupid Con."

"I love your little pet names." He was leaning back in the sand, picking his teeth with a fish bone. "God, isn't this great? A friggin' island paradise with a beautiful woman who brings me food and cooks and has a great set of—never mind."

"Are you talking about my 'rack' again?"

"Uh, yeah. Sorry."

"*I* don't mind. I am the one breaking your nudity taboo. Besides, you have a nice rack, too." And he did. Shirtless, she could see the tanned skin, the firm muscles, the light fuzz of chest hair that tapered down to a straight line leading to his groin.

He laughed. “Oh, darlin’, you’re gonna get in trouble if you keep talking like that.”

“You mean you might like to mate with me?”

He choked on the fish bone.

Chapter 12

"It's all right," she hastily assured him after pounding him on the back and extracting the bone. "I don't expect you to mate with me. Why would you ever want to?"

That was enough of *that* crap, he decided, and seized her by the back of the neck, yanked her close, and kissed her. She was so surprised her mouth popped open, which delighted him, and he plunged his tongue inside. Given that he hadn't brushed his teeth in a few days (and who knew if mermaids did?) the kiss was amazing.

He eased her down on the sand and did what he had been longing to do since he'd first seen her: pounced on her breasts. The breath popped out of her lungs (gills?) as she laughed, and then gasped when he sucked a pale pink nipple into his mouth.

He lavished attention on her creamy mounds, licking, nibbling, sucking, and even (very, very gently) biting. Beneath him she wriggled in the sand and clutched his shoulders with surprising strength. In fact, he was fairly certain he'd have bruises. Not that he gave a good damn.

He slipped his hand between her cool, chubby thighs and she parted her legs and pulled him to her as he thrust into her moist warmth. Her thighs gripped him, again with that astonishing strength, and she rose to meet him. Now they were both gasping and groaning in each other's arms, and he cut his tongue on one of her teeth and didn't care.

"Oh—you're—bleeding—"

"Don't—care," he gasped.

"Sorry—sorry—maybe we—should—stop?"

"Shut. Up."

This time he didn't think it was an accident when

his tongue got punctured, but he had it coming so that was all right. In fact, it was so all right he laughed into her mouth, a noise which was instantly cut off as she tightened all over (*all* over) and shivered with the force of her orgasm.

That sent him right over the edge, and he knew it was going to be no use thinking about baseball or saying the alphabet backward. He came so hard he actually shuddered from heels to throat, and then unceremoniously collapsed over her.

Chapter 13

After about ten minutes had passed, Reanesta worried he had passed out, or was bleeding to death from a punctured tongue. So she tapped him on the shoulder.

"Sleepy," he yawned against her throat.

"I am a patient woman, as I think you have noticed. But you're squashing me."

He snorted, but rolled off her—and yelped when he nearly rolled into the fire, which had burned down to embers. He tossed a few more sticks on, then said, "Where the hell did my jeans go?"

"Oh. I, uh, was, um, anxious to, ah, mate with you before you changed your mind." She held up denim shreds. "I do apologize."

"You did this with your *hands*? Jesus!"

"I apologize," she said again, blushing.

"No, shit, it's impressive as hell, I'm not bitching. About this, I mean."

She giggled. "A welcome change."

He stuck his tongue out at her. "Ith it ee'ing?"

"Not anymore."

"We're going to have to practice French kissing."

"We are?" she asked, delighted.

"Shit, yeah. Otherwise it could get downright dangerous. You don't see a blood bank on this island, do you?"

"Very well. We shall practice."

"Starting right now," he said, and pounced on her like a big land cat.

"Again?" she asked, delighted. "You wish to mate again?"

He sighed. "Ree, I've never known a woman so strong, smart, efficient, rude, and dumb at the same time."

"Thank you?"

"Even if you weren't gorgeous—which you *are*—you'd be a catch for any man. And I'd think that even if you hadn't saved my ass. Multiple times," he admitted.

"You're so nice, Con."

"I get off on being 'nice,'" he said dryly. "In fact, I feel like being 'nice' right now."

And he was. Extremely nice.

Chapter 14

The next few days passed like a dream. A hot sex dream in which he was the star and the prettiest woman in the world was his costar. (He *had* to stop thinking in terms of movies and television.)

They bathed together, walked to the freshwater stream together, and she started to teach him to swim. She also disappeared periodically and returned with fish, which they cooked and ate.

He tried not to worry about her—in fact, given that

he'd seen her in action it was stupid to worry about her—but couldn't help it. The ocean was a big place. What if—what if a *bunch* of sharks ganged up on her? What if she ran into a bunch of merman bullies?

So he was always relieved to see her return, and she was always surprised at his relief. And she always said the same thing before she disappeared: "I will come back."

He missed his show, but had to admit that life on a deserted island with Ree was a pretty damned nice consolation prize.

They made love as often as humanly (mermanly?) possible; he didn't think he would ever get tired of her body. And she was indefatigable, not to mention inventive and uninhibited. He supposed a culture that swam around naked probably didn't have a lot of hang-ups about sex.

They gorged on fish and coconuts and she occasionally brought him fistfuls of that odd, puffy seaweed. He longed for a steak, or a burger and a beer, but again, life with Ree on the island had plenty of advantages.

And one big disadvantage.

After about a week, he tackled the problem that was troubling him. "Ree, it's not that I'm not grateful—"

"Oh, dear, more of your 'bitching.'"

"—and it's not that I'm not loving our time here, because I am."

"I can tell," she said, smiling and pointing at his groin. He'd decided nudity was the way to go as well, but had saved his boxers and T-shirt . . . for what, he wasn't sure.

"Stop that, I'm being serious. But Ree, how long are you going to stay with me? Don't you have a family . . . people worried about you?"

"No."

"So you're just going to . . . I mean, I might never get rescued."

"Are you suggesting I just swim off and leave you?" she said, aghast.

"Well. Uh. I don't *want* you to leave—"

"I thought you liked me." Oh, Christ! Was that—it was! A *tear* was trickling down her left cheek.

"Ree! I do like you, I adore you, I worship you!" He pulled her into his arms and, luckily, she decided to be pulled (he had estimated that she was at least twice as strong as he was). "But this isn't any kind of life for you. I'm just saying I don't expect you to give up everything to stay on this little spit of sand for God knows how long."

"I'm not leaving you," she said, her voice muffled against his chest.

"All right, all right. Quit cryin', will ya?" He was in a near panic. He hadn't thought she had tear ducts! "I'm glad you want to stay, okay? It's just . . . something that's been on my mind for a bit, that's all."

So that was settled, and things went on as they had: idyllic and fun and lots of sex.

For a while.

Chapter 15

About a week later, Ree came striding out of the waves looking distracted and carrying five fish.

"Run into trouble?"

"Not . . . exactly."

"What's *that* mean?" he said, spitting the fish.

"I think—I think I heard someone. One of my folk. So I—so I called him."

"Oh."

"Perhaps he can aid in your rescue."

"*Oh.*" He thought that over for a second. "Jeez, thanks! I guess it's a long shot, but thanks for trying."

"Mmmm."

She was distracted the rest of the morning, and although he got the shock of his life when a man with vivid green hair and purple (purple!) eyes strode out of the waves, Ree only looked resigned.

"Greetings, Reanesta," he said in a deep baritone, naked as a newt. "Were you calling me? I am Jertan."

"Yes." Instead of shaking hands, they sort of clasped each other's elbows. "Thank you for coming. This is my—my friend, Con."

"Hello, Con." Jertan looked curious and (odd, given that he was a good three inches taller and at least thirty pounds heavier, all of it muscle) even a little wary. Con reminded himself that the Undersea Folk (for so Ree called them) were new to walking up to ordinary folks. "Are you the biped Conwin Edmund Conlinson?"

Con felt his eyebrows arch in surprise. "Yeah." He stuck out a hand and Jertan shook it carefully. Con took his hand back, relieved none of his fingers had been crushed. "How'd you know?"

"Why, many bipeds are searching for you! They fear you have been lost forever. When I see," he added, with a sly look at Ree, "that you are in fact doing quite well for yourself."

"Watch it," he said mildly.

Jertan grinned, showing the same startlingly sharp teeth Ree had. "I will indeed. In fact, I will return to my home on the mainland and give them the coordinates of this island."

"That's—thanks."

"Our people must learn to get along," Jertan said carelessly. "Reanesta, may I be of further assistance?"

"No, Jertan," she said colorlessly. "It was kind of you to come."

"Courtesy to my folk is no kindness. I am going now," he said, and without another word turned and walked back into the surf.

"You guys really aren't into saying good-bye, are you?" he asked, watching the guy disappear into the waves.

Ree shrugged.

"Well!" he boomed with false cheer. "You'll be rid of me in a few days. That should be a load off your mind."

"Yes, indeed."

"Pretty soon you'll be free, and I'll be back on TV."

"Yes."

Then why did he have such a sick feeling in his stomach, and why did she look so strange?

Chapter 16

The rescue boat showed up three days later. Reanesta watched it, wondering if she might vomit. Could she be carrying Con's pup? She'd been ill the last few mornings, but it was too soon to tell—and frankly, just the thought of Con disappearing forever was enough to make her feel ill. And she would fight a thousand great whites before trying to keep him on the island when he so obviously wanted to get back to his life. His show.

His stupid, silly survivor show. *Survivor! Ha!*

Con was waving madly, having hurriedly dressed in his shorts and shirt. The large boat honked twice in response, anchored, and then she could see men preparing to lower a smaller boat into the water.

"I don't want them to see me," she told him quietly. "I will leave now."

"Wha—now? *Now* now? But I wanted to introduce you to my crew!"

"I," she replied, "do not wish to see them."

"Oh." He rubbed his jaw, which was sporting a reddish brown beard after all this time. "Like that, huh? Done with your little pet project, now?"

She didn't know what he was talking about. *He* was the one who couldn't wait to leave. "I will not be back," she said, and turned to leave.

"Wait!" he snarled, snatching her elbow. She coolly considered breaking his wrist and decided that would be unusually—what was the word? *Bitchy.* "Jeez, you just can't wait to get out of here, can you? I gave you the chance last week! You said you wanted to stay with me."

"And you," she said coldly, "love your show more than you love any living creature." Couldn't he see her pride? Didn't he understand she couldn't ask him to give up his life to stay with her? "Now remove your hand, before I remove your lungs."

He let go of her like she was hot. "Fine," he snapped. "Thanks for saving my life and for all the sex."

"You are most welcome," she replied icily and walked around to the far end of the island where the small boat couldn't see her, and when she hit the water it was a great relief because the salt water nicely camouflaged her tears.

Chapter 17

"Con! Babe! We're all set to start shooting for sweeps. Your comeback is going to be *the* lead for the week. We've already sold all the ad time," Alan, his producer, burbled.

"Super."

"Con! Babe! You've been moping ever since we picked you up off of that godforsaken island."

"Don't call it that," he snapped. "It was a very nice island."

"Con! Babe! *What* is your *damage*? Although thank heavens you finally shaved; that mountain man look was just too awful."

"Nothin'," he muttered. They were lounging in his trailer, it was six days later, and he was belatedly realizing that leaving Ree behind was the biggest fucking mistake he had ever made—and that included getting his sorry self shipwrecked in the first place. "Got a lot on my mind."

"I can *imagine*. After your *dreadful* experience, which of course we'll re-create so you can show the audience how you survived—"

He sat bolt upright, and Alan's watery blue eyes, magnified behind the glasses he affected to make him look older than his twenty-six years, widened. "That's just it, Alan. I didn't survive. I mean, I did, but only because a mermaid helped me."

"A"—Alan goggled—"a real live mermaid? One of those Undersea Folk they're talking about on CNN?"

"Yeah. Her name was Ree and she saved my life about nine times. Towed me to that island where you found me. Telepathically called for help and this guy named Jertan came to the rescue, which is how you heard where I was. She did *everything* for me. And I—I just left her there." He buried his face in his hands. "I left her."

Alan's hand was on his shoulder. "It sounds like you two got kind of close."

"I sort of fell in love with her," he said hollowly, "when she bit the hammerhead."

"When she did what? Never mind. Let's find her!"

"Find her?" Alan's enthusiasm could be exhausting. "She's long gone. She lives all over the world, all by herself. And the ocean's a big damn place."

"We'll use the show," Alan said excitedly, actually jumping from one foot to the other. His blond hair fell into his eyes and he shook it back. "Every show, you'll open by talking about—Ree, was it?—by talking about her and asking people to help you find her. Cripes, the guy she called for help—maybe he watches the show!"

"He did know who I was," Con said thoughtfully. "I didn't even get a chance to introduce myself."

"There you go!"

Con felt cautious optimism. “It’s worth a shot.”

“Great! I’ll go tell the writers to redo the opening.”

“Oh, they’ll love that.”

“They will obey or be killed,” Alan said cheerfully, pushing his glasses up on his nose. “You watch. This will work.”

Chapter 18

This is Con 'Bad Baby' Conlinson and yup, I'm back. I'm just like you . . . only I'm on TV. I've gotten really close to the summit of Everest, spent the night in the Everglades (Motel™), faced down numerous angry dogs and cats, gotten thrown out of no less than seven—*seven*—bars, surfed the insanity of Lake Ontario, stayed dry in Seattle, and been audited twice.

"And now I'm back after being shipwrecked for a

couple of weeks, and I'll show you how to survive like I did. But first, I need you to bear with me 'cuz I've got some personal business to clear up.

"I want to tell Ree that I love her and I'm sorry I left and I want to marry her if she'll only agree to live with me. We'll vacation all over the world, you can come on the show if you want, or not, and wherever we go we'll make sure there's salt water nearby.

"Y'see, folks, I didn't survive on my own at all. A beautiful mermaid named Ree helped me. She saved my life. She fought off a hammerhead shark for me, and made me eat raw fish so I wouldn't die like a dog in that rotten rowboat. I owe her my life, and I was stupid to leave her when I got rescued. She's the *real* survival expert, and I'm really hoping she'll agree to forgive me for leaving and come on the show and show y'all how to get along in the middle of the ocean.

"So, if anyone out there watching knows Ree—her real name's Reanesta and she has silver hair, silver eyes, and a silver tail—could you please tell her to get in touch with me? We'll run my contact information in a constant stream, as you can see, on the bottom of your screen. And Jertan, if you're watching, I'll be your slave forever if you get word to Ree that I miss her and I need her.

"Well, thanks, folks, for putting up with that. Now let's get to the season opener of *Con Con the Survivin' Man.*"

Chapter 19

After the show had been airing for two weeks, Con decided Ree wasn't coming. Well, that was her prerogative, and it wasn't like he didn't have it coming, leaving her like that for his stupid *career*. He got the shakes every time he thought of how stupid he'd been, how he'd thrown happiness away with both hands and never even looked back. Stupid Con! Ree had been right all along.

"Con?"

But he was going to keep up the appeals, and if

the crew had a betting pool he was pretending not to notice, and if his producer was starting to think it was time for a new angle, he didn't give a shit.

"Con?"

"No autographs right now, hon," he said, walking by whoever-it-was. No, he couldn't worry about fans right now, his heart was breaking and he was—

"Stupid Con!"

He whirled on his heels and—there was Ree!

"You're wearing clothes," he gasped. "No wonder I didn't recognize you."

"Well, I could hardly come to your set in my usual manner," she said. "May I have some water? I'm dreadfully thirsty."

"You—water? Water! Right!" He seized her hand, thinking that he preferred her nude, although she looked nice in her jeans, sandals, and dark blue T-shirt. Her silver hair was pinned up; he preferred it down. Cripes, he'd been aching for her for weeks and had *walked right by her*. He wondered briefly where she got the clothes, then dragged her to his trailer.

Once inside he seized her and kissed her until they were both gasping. Then he fished around in the fridge and handed her two bottles of water, which she glugged in twenty seconds.

"Oh, thank you. *Much* better. Also, I am carrying your pup."

"My—you're pregnant?"

"Yes. And I thought you said lovely things about me on your show. And you must be Jertan's slave, because he told me you were looking for me. How he found me off the coast of Fiji I'll never know," she added in a mutter, "but he did. And here I am."

"You're *pregnant*?"

"Yes." She eyed him warily, silver eyes narrowing. "That troubles you? You do not wish a half-breed child?"

"Troubles me?" He whooped and spun around in a circle. "I've got you now, Ree! You're stuck with me forever! Ha!"

"That is sweet," she said. But she looked doubtful.

"Well, shit, you don't seem very fuckin' excited about it!"

"I do not wish to trap you, or make you give up your lifestyle. And I am willing to live with you and be your mate—more than willing. But I need the sea,

Con. I need to see it, smell it, be in it, every day. Or I'll die, as you would have died."

"No problem," he promised instantly. "We'll move the studio to the California coast. We don't have to stay in Alabama. And you can come on-site whenever you want."

"I shall have to," she said dryly, "if only to make sure the father of my pup doesn't expire of dehydration, malnutrition, or shark attack."

"You can be my costar," he said eagerly. "You're the real survival expert. I've been telling everybody that."

"Yes, I saw." She smiled at him. "That's why I came back. When you admitted your—ah—failings. To your audience. And your crew. I do not require credit. You may be the survival expert in the family, and the television star. But if you ever leave me again, I will hunt you down and break your silly biped legs."

"Agreed," he promised fervently. "Great. No problem. Man, wait'll I tell my mom! Will the baby be a mermaid, too?"

"I do not know," she replied. "I only know she—

yes, it's a girl—will be part me, and part you. And I never knew I wanted that, until I had it."

He snatched her to him and kissed her again, then let go like she was radioactive. "Oh, shit! Did I hurt the baby when I did that?"

"I hate to tell you this, but the baby will likely be stronger than you the moment she reaches her weaning year." Then, "You have a mother?"

"Yup."

"Oh."

"Don't worry, she'll love you. And so will all my brothers and sisters."

"All your—how many—"

"Seven."

She sat down as if all the strength had gone out of her legs. "But I don't know how to be in a family!" she wailed. "My folk died when I was still in my nursing year!"

"Well, babe, it's time you learned. You didn't think I was gonna let you wander the ocean alone forever, didja?"

"Well. For a little while, yes." She smiled again.

"But then I saw your show. I almost didn't recognize you without the beard."

"And I didn't even notice you with your hair up and clothes on. Which reminds me"—he pointed—"off!"

She obliged, seeming happy to be rid of the clothing, and unpinned her hair, and he pounced on her. Then he hesitated. "This won't hurt the baby, will it?"

"Stupid Con," she said, and kissed him so hard, his mouth was bruised for three days.

Speed Dating, Werewolf Style

Or, Ow, I Think You Broke the Bone

There is no silver bullet and frankly you probably don't need one. It is far more important to be able to find the right kind of gun, be able to load the gun . . . and perhaps most importantly, be able to figure out where the werewolf is.

—MATTHEW OLIPHANT, *USEABILITY WORKS*

★

The werewolf is neither man nor wolf, but a satanic creature with the worst qualities of both.

—JOHN COLTON, *STUART WALKER*

★

The werewolf instinctively seeks to kill the thing it loves best.

—JOHN COLTON, *STUART WALKER*

I have led her home, my love, my only friend.
There is none like her, none.
And never yet so warmly ran my blood
And sweetly, on and on
Calming itself to the long-wished-for end
Full to the banks, close on the promised good.

—ALFRED TENNYSON,
TENNYSON, A SELECTED EDITION

★

There's no such thing as a werewolf.

—ERIC SINCLAIR, VAMPIRE KING

For all the Wyndham werewolf fans out there, this one's for you. And yes, I'll probably do another single title one of these days. You know, when I kick my booze and prescription pill habit.

Author's Note

The events of this novella take place four days after the events in *Undead and Uneasy*.

Chapter 1

Most people wouldn't know a werewolf if said werewolf (literally) bit them in the face.

Werewolves look like you or me; perhaps a bit more muscular, yes, and their reflexes are much quicker, but it is the nature of man to not notice such things, and so . . . most people wouldn't know a werewolf if they saw one.

Not so with Cain.

Cain just looked *wrong*. Your brain registered it,

even if the eye did not. She was short, almost petite—barely five feet tall. She wore her coffee-colored hair brutally short, in a buzz cut that emphasized her sharp cheekbones. She tended to run around in jeans and tank-tops, which showed off her smoothly muscled legs and arms.

Most arresting of all, she had a sharp, fox-like face, with a pointed chin and glaring green eyes. Cat green. And some people described them as poison green.

A striking woman who moved just a little too quickly, who seemed a little too strong for her size. A small woman who ate two steaks a night, just about every night. And multiple raw eggs for breakfast.

Yes. Something wrong. Even if you couldn't quite put your finger on it.

Cain was pondering this phenomenon as the mugger, who was over a foot taller and several pounds heavier, got a good look at her eyes, dropped the knife, and fled. She hadn't even had to say anything. She had just looked at him.

She bent and picked the knife up off the street, wary of some tourists stepping on it and hurting themselves, snapped off the blade, and dropped both pieces into a nearby trash can.

She'd been back on-Cape for just a couple of days and already some idiot tried to *mug* her? On the *Cape*?

She had decided long ago that she would never fit in—except, of course, with the Pack, and what else mattered?—so why bother trying? It's not like the monkeys ever paid attention. They stayed away from her or they ignored her. Or they tried to mug her—apparently that was the new thing.

For this reason she had never once left Cape Cod, not in twenty-nine years.

Except once.

Which was why she was in her current predicament.

Antonia, the unbelievably bitchy werewolf (except she was a freak; she never changed . . . she saw the future instead) who had taken off for Minnesota ages ago, had gone missing.

And Michael, their Pack leader, had instantly formed a small group to hunt her up. He had politely invited Cain to join them—except with Michael, a polite request wasn't really a request at all. And so she had gone.

And seeing all her old friends again, catching up on their lives, she had been amazed to find them all . . . *settled*. Domesticated, even.

Jon had been bad enough, but then Michael . . . and Derik . . . and Brendan . . . they were all happily mated and having cubs, for God's sake.

And they had grown up together, had been cubs together, and had sworn not to settle down before age thirty. Now they were *all* settled, and she was the only single one, and damned if her competitive streak wasn't kicking in. Now she had until her thirtieth birthday to find a mate.

In other words, she had twenty-two days.

Cain irrationally blamed the entire thing on the vampire queen, because if *she* had been able to keep her house in order, Cain would never have been forced to face certain facts she'd been successfully ignoring by living in Provincetown . . . as far from Wyndham Manor as she could get without actually leaving the Cape.

So the hunt was on. Time to find a Pack member who needed a mate and didn't mind a quickie wedding.

How she was going to do this, she had no idea. Thus, the late-night stroll to clear her head. The only man in her life so far had been the mugger.

Stupid vampire queen.

Chapter 2

"I need to find a mate," she announced to her oldest friend, Saul, who froze with a forkful of clam linguine halfway to his mouth. "Right now."

"And you're, uh, telling me why?"

"Because you know a lot of guys, and I don't. You've got to help me hook up."

Her only single friend blinked at her as he chewed his pasta. She had known him forever—they had been babies in the crib together, their mothers had been best friends—and they always told each other everything.

When he'd left the Cape after they graduated high school she had been afraid he would never return, but they'd stayed in touch with weekly phone calls and after he got his degree in engineering from (of all places!) the University of Wisconsin, he had come back and settled into a job at Excel Engineering. Within five years he was the number two man there.

It didn't surprise her. Saul had always been brilliant around machines and gears and things. It was people who gave him trouble. He had a tendency to stammer when nervous or angry, didn't seem to know what to do with his long arms and legs at parties, and, in short, was a classic beta male.

That wasn't to say he wasn't pretty cute, because he was. Tall and lean, with a shock of black hair that tended to fall into his eyes at inopportune moments, and chocolate brown eyes. At least *he* had stuck to their deal, because otherwise some bim would have snatched him up ages ago. He'd be a *great* husband for some lucky woman. Hmm. Maybe after she was settled, she'd think about fixing him up with somebody. Problem was, he was her only real friend, she didn't really know a lot of—

"Why the big rush to find a mate?" he asked after swallowing.

"Haven't you noticed? *All* our old friends are mated and most of them have cubs, even! So much," she added bitterly, "for swearing to stay single until at least thirty."

"Yeah," he said, idly spinning his fork in the pasta. "I had noticed."

"Right!" She plopped down in the kitchen chair opposite him. Saul had inherited a beautiful house on 6A from his parents; it was big enough to be a bed and breakfast, but Saul made plenty of dough at Excel. It was a bitch to get to in the summer (awful, *awful* tourists), but worth the trip every time. She felt more at home here than at her apartment in P-town. "So now *I've* gotta get married by the time I'm thirty."

"But that's three weeks away."

"I knowwwwwww. Thus, the 'right away' comment. Remember, when I came in?"

"Yeah, I remember. It was forty seconds ago."

"Okay, then!" She slapped the flat of her hand on his table. "So hook me up. Maybe we can set up one of those speed-dating things, except with werewolves."

"Or maybe," he said, after chewing another forkful, "you could set aside your ruthless competitive streak for once."

"Fat chance of *that* happening. It's me, Saul, Cain. Remember?"

He sighed. She picked up a napkin and wiped a dab of garlic sauce off his chin. "Yeah. I remember. Stop that, you're not my mother."

"Aw, Saul." She tweaked his chin. "I'm practically your sister, and you know it."

He snorted. "I've got enough problems without having you as a sibling. That would complicate my life enormously. And you've already done that, and you haven't been here a minute." He snorted again. "Speed dating."

"Aw, come on. I know you can do it. We'll set it up at Finnegan's."

"Forever to be known in the future as Hell on Earth."

"Will you stop being such a crybaby and help me?"

He sighed. "Yes. And yes."

She beamed. "Good boy. And you've got sauce on your cheek."

Chapter 3

Candidate number one sat across from her at her table in the back corner of Finnegan's, her and Saul's favorite bar in Orleans. And immediately sneezed into his drink.

"Sorry," he said, whipping out a *cloth* handkerchief and (ecch!) blowing his nose in it, then stuffing it back into his jacket pocket. "Allergies."

"But you're a werewolf!"

"Half. On my mom's side. And the pollen's murder this time of—" He sneezed again and a glob of snot actually landed on her arm. Before she could break a chair over his head, he had mopped it up with his damp handkerchief.

"Next!" she called. She wasn't even going to give this guy the full minute, so she reset the timer.

Candidate number two sat down, clutching two orange drinks—she assumed they were screwdrivers—and frantically waving the waitress down for a third. In thirty seconds he had gulped both drinks, and had the flushed cheeks and bloodshot eyes of a closet drunk. It took a *lot* of booze to get a werewolf drunk, but he was managing nicely.

"Next!"

Candidate number three sat down, eyed her, then said disapprovingly, "What have you done to your hair? It's much too short. You've got to grow it longer."

"Next!"

"You're not even giving them the full minute," Saul murmured in her ear, making her jump. For a gawky, gangly engineer, he moved like a matador.

"Oh, boy, are you gonna get it when we get back to your place. I can't believe you picked these guys!"

"Your gratitude is overwhelming."

"Get lost, here comes number four."

Saul glided away as number four sat down across from her . . . and instantly pulled out a pack of cigarettes. "Mind?"

"Yeah, actually." She couldn't abide the smell of cigarette smoke; most werewolves couldn't. She was amazed he'd picked up the habit.

"Well, this is me, baby."

"Don't call me baby. Next!"

Candidate number five sat down and instantly started nibbling on his nails, a filthy monkey habit almost as bad as smoking.

"How do you hunt," she asked, fascinated, "if you keep eating your claws?"

"Nervous tic."

"Yeah, well, it's kind of skeeving me out."

He nibbled harder. "It gets worse when I'm under stress. Which you're definitely putting me under."

"Pal, you haven't *seen* stress. Next!"

"That's it," Saul said.

"What?" she cried. "Only five? Five losers?"

"You gave me," he reminded her, "twenty hours notice."

"Oh, sure, it's *my* fault. Man, if I didn't know you so well I'd swear you set me up with those idiots on purpose."

"Now why would I do that?" he asked mildly, sitting down across from her. "You can just call me candidate number six."

"Very fucking funny, Saul. So now what do we do?"

"Have a drink?"

"After that. My birthday loometh."

"Well, I did fix you up for a blind date tomorrow night."

"Excellent!"

"Yeah," he said, draining his beer. "Excellent."

Chapter 4

Is that what you're wearing?" Saul asked as soon as she walked into his living room. He had all kinds of incomprehensible paperwork spread around him, and looked harassed.

She looked down at herself. Clean denim shorts, a navy blue T-shirt. Black suede flats. It was July on Cape Cod; what *else* would she wear? "What? What's wrong with it?"

"What if he's planning to take you somewhere nice?"

She scowled at him. "I'm not wearing a dress or a skirt and that is *that.*"

He sighed. "You're not making this very easy."

"Hey, I *never* said it would be easy."

"Yes, you've been threatening me with that since kindergarten."

"What's all the stuff?" she asked, kneeling beside him. "Work junk?"

"Work junk," he agreed. "New client. Place is a disaster. I foresee a month of twenty-hour days. Especially now that you've dumped your little project on me."

"Bitch, bitch, bitch," she said good-naturedly. "Hey, maybe you can fix me up with some of your clients."

"We only have three werewolves, and they're all mated."

"Rats."

"'Rats' as in 'Oh, rats' or rats as in 'They're rats to be married'?"

She pondered that one for a moment, then finally said, "Both." She looked around at all the paperwork with distaste. "Saul, when was the last time you had a vacation?"

"What year is it?"

"If you have to ask, it's been too damn long."

He shrugged. "I like my work."

"Yeah, that's fine, but you should think about settling down, too. You don't want to be the only one in the old gang not mated."

"God forbid," he said dryly. "Plague and famine would be more welcome." There was a polite rap on his door. "Ah. Prince Charming has arrived."

"Please God," Cain said fervently, and went to answer the door.

Chapter 5

"My patients are really my life, and they're all so different, that's what I love about my work, the constant variety, I mean, every single day is different—"

Oh my God. This guy hasn't stopped talking since he picked me up at Saul's.

"—Dr. Williams is *so* arrogant, he just won't tolerate any nurses, thinks we're all trained monkeys—badly trained monkeys—and—"

Jesus. He's never going to stop talking.

"—and then there was Mrs. Jenkins, boy, she was a firecracker! D'you know she was friends with Michael's mother? Man, the stories she told! They were—"

I'm going to have to kill him and escape.

"—of course, what I'd really like is to go back to school and become a nurse practitioner. With the national nursing shortage, I can pretty much—"

Should I hit him until he shuts up? With what? A fire extinguisher?

"—they can write prescriptions and the money's really great, not to mention—"

I'll hit Saul. That's what I'll do.

"—you're really great to talk to, you know how to listen, which I really—"

First this guy, then Saul, then myself. A double murder/suicide.

"—work such long hours, it's so hard to meet people, but of course it's worth it for the job, I mean, it's just so rewarding—"

Oh my God. Where is that waitress? I need another drink so badly.

"—couldn't believe it when Saul called me up and said you wanted to go out, I mean, we've all wondered why you haven't settled down—"

At this rate, I'll be unmated when I'm fifty.

"—then you had that cool mission to Minnesota, something about Antonia and—can this be right?—a vampire queen? I mean, it's like something out of a Stephen King novel—"

Stupid vampire queen.

Chapter 6

"Come on," Saul said, setting a plate of steak and fries in front of her, along with a glass of six raw eggs. Among other things, Saul was a good cook and knew all her favorites.

"What, come on? It was awful!"

It was eleven o'clock at night; her date had ended early. Except it hadn't felt early, God no.

Saul was unruffled. "It couldn't have been that bad."

"He *never* shut up! It was work, work, work, and

blah, blah, blah—he doesn't know a thing about me because I couldn't get a word in edgewise!"

"He's single, makes a good living, good-looking (not that I see him that way), and wants to settle down."

"No, he's looking for a blow-up doll that will listen all day and all night. God!" She drained her glass of eggs in three swallows. "I didn't think I'd ever get out of there."

"Well, you did. And here you are. Again."

"You never used to mind when I dropped by," she grumped. She chewed her steak furiously, then said, "You look like hell. You're working too hard. Take a damned vacation already."

He shrugged. "From what? Excel, or you?"

"You're hilarious."

"The good news—if you can call it that—is that I've set you up with another date for tomorrow night. Word's getting around that you're looking to settle down."

"Excellent! There's no way this guy can be worse than the other six."

"You really do like to jinx yourself, don't you?"

"Nuh-uh! Okay, maybe that was a dumb thing to

say. I guess we'll wait and see how it goes tomorrow night." She chewed another piece. Then: "Word's really getting around?"

He shrugged and flipped his black hair out of his eyes. "You know how our kind are. We're genetically inclined to settle down young and have cubs. So the news that the infamous Cain, single for almost thirty years—"

"Because of the pact!"

"—wanting to settle down is pretty good gossip."

"A dream come true. I'm gossip fodder."

"There's worse things," he said, and cracked two more eggs into her glass.

Chapter 7

She didn't care for number seven—Geoff Ren—and she couldn't put her finger on why.

Certainly he was smooth, and handsome (in a distant, icy blond, blue-eyed way), and charming. He listened to her, courteously offered to move them away from a cigarette smoker, and sent her steak back when it showed up overcooked. He made sure her drink glass was always full, and offered to take her somewhere else for dessert when nothing really grabbed her on the menu.

Maybe he was a little too—controlling?

Stop it, she scolded herself. *You'll never get mated at this rate. Now you're just* looking *for reasons to reject these guys. Geoff's been a great date. The best of a bad lot, that's for damn sure.*

They had pulled up to Saul's house in his Lexus hybrid, and she turned to him to say, "Maybe we could get together tom—" when all of a sudden he'd yanked her toward him (breaking her seat belt) and mashed his mouth down on hers.

Outraged and startled, she tried to shove him away. When that didn't work (he was over six feet tall, and much, much stronger), she bit him.

"Ouch! You little *bitch*. Why did you come out if you didn't want some?"

"It's our first date, Geoff, you ass! Jeez, I'm gonna have a friction burn on my neck from the seat belt."

"You'll heal," he snapped, then snatched at her again, this time shoving his tongue into her mouth. Her back slammed against the steering wheel and there was a sonorous *honk*. His hands groped, reached, grabbed, and she could feel him yanking at her bra.

She fumbled for the driver's side door handle and,

when the door swung open, tumbled out and hit the pavement with a teeth-rattling thud.

He jumped out, his legs landing on either side of her back, and she scrambled to get away from him. He caught the back of her T-shirt and she wrenched away, hearing the fabric tear.

"Cut the shit!" she yelled, only to hit the side of the Lexus with a bang when the back of his hand caught her full across the jaw. God, he was fast! She hadn't even seen his arm move. "Geoff, stop it!"

"*You* stop it, you fucking cocktease."

Well, at least now she could put her finger on what was wrong with number seven.

For the thousandth time she blessed her size, as she slithered down the side of the car and scooted underneath, out of reach of his grasping hands. She scrambled across the tarmac and emerged on the other side of the car. Saul's front door was only twenty feet away.

She'd only gotten five steps when he tackled her from behind. Her face banged into the lawn and she felt blood start to trickle from her nose. He flipped her over—and caught her fist on the point of his chin. In return he gave her an eye-watering slap. So she reached down, groping for his crotch.

"Now you're getting with the program," he grunted. "That's—eeeeeeee-yowwwwww!" She'd found his balls, and squeezed so hard she felt the veins pop up on her forearm.

Then, suddenly, he was yanked off her, and Saul, oh thank God, Saul was there, holding the guy by the scruff of his neck like a puppy.

"Oh, Christ, my balls, oh my fucking balls, Jesus, I gotta get to a hospital, agh, my balls!" Geoff writhed and moaned at the end of Saul's arm.

"Then let m-me assist y-you to your car," Saul said, and *threw* Geoff into the side of the Lexus. The car door actually dented and Geoff flopped to the pavement, unconscious.

"Are y-you okay, C–cain?"

She sat up and spat to get the blood out of her mouth. "Wow," she said. "Saul. Jeez. Didn't think you had it in you."

Then she burst into tears.

Chapter 8

Cain woke up the next morning in her room. Well, not her room, the room at Saul's she always stayed in when she slept over. She'd been having sleepovers in this house for twenty-five years.

Saul must have heard her stirring—he had ears like a lynx—because there was a gentle rap at the door.

"C'mon in," she yawned, stretched. She had slept in one of Saul's old shirts and her underpants; her T-shirt, of course, had been ruined.

He poked his head in. "Sleep okay?"

"Like a rock."

"Christ!"

"What?"

He crossed the room and put a finger under her chin, tipping her face up. "You've already got a shiner. That fucker." For Saul, that was big talk. "Should have kicked in his ribs, too."

"I'm pretty sure I ruptured his sack," she said, gingerly feeling her left eye and wincing. *Yep. Puffy, swollen, and probably a lovely purple black.* "And I'm pretty sure you fractured his skull. Trust me, he's hurting way worse this morning. My bruises will heal up in a day or two."

He sat down on the edge of her bed. "I don't think you should do this anymore," he said abruptly, squinting at her.

"Granted, it hasn't been going well," she said dryly.

"You know how I said word was getting around that you wanted a mate? I think some guys are interpreting that as you want to get laid. Case in point: Geoff the asshole."

She smirked. "Is that his family name?"

"Cain. I'm being serious."

"I'm not letting Geoff the asshole scare me off the dating scene. It was a temporary setback at best."

"Temporary setback?" Saul practically yelled. "Y-you almost got r-raped!"

"Calm down, you're going to give yourself a stroke. Besides, you swung to the rescue like—like frickin' Tarzan or something. I must admit, Saul, I didn't think you could surprise me anymore."

"You never think that," he grumbled.

She yawned again. "So what's on the agenda for tonight?"

"You're taking tonight off," he said firmly.

"Spoilsport."

"Damn right."

"Saul, I'm *fine*."

"You didn't l-look fine last n-night."

She thought about it. Screaming, punching, and, finally, crying. The overwhelming strength of Geoff, how he wouldn't listen, how she had been fairly powerless against him. The hits. The things he had said.

Yeah. Saul had a point.

"But I had you to come to the rescue," she teased,

putting her hand on his. "I'm the one usually saving your ass."

"So. I owed you one."

"Actually, if we're gonna go back to kindergarten, you owe me about fifty."

"Well, I sure as shit don't want to even up!" he yelled, face reddening.

"You've *really* got to take a vacation. You're so stressed!"

"Is it any fucking wonder? Your social life is killing me."

"Stop exaggerating. What's for breakfast?"

He collapsed next to her. "I hate you."

"Aw, you know you can't resist me. Breakfast?"

"More than life itself, I hate you."

"Pancakes and bacon?" she asked hopefully. "And eggs? And maybe a pork chop?"

"You know, most women, after being assaulted, would be, I don't know, traumatized? Not looking for a damned pork chop!"

"Well," she said reasonably, "if you don't have one, we can always heat up the leftover steak."

Chapter 9

As usual, she had a ton more fun with Saul than all her other dates put together, multiplied by ten. They had a terrific dinner, most of which he made on the patio grill, chased with several ice-cold Coronas. Then they watched *Shaun of the Dead*, *Hot Fuzz*, and *300*—*300* being her favorite movie of all time.

"My God," Saul commented, munching popcorn. They were sitting together on the couch in front of the TV. "This movie is made for women and gay men. Look at the abs on all those guys."

"You have abs like that."

"Yeah, but I'm an unnatural creature of moonlight. Most men do not look like that. It's kind of cruel, really. To do this to the women and the gay men."

She laughed and drained her third beer. "You think any of the cast is Pack?"

"They must be. *Look* at them."

"Wouldn't the producer just shit?"

"What a vivid mental image, my dear."

"Oh, here it comes! He's gonna throw the spear at that creepy fucking Xerxes. You *believe* the guy playing Xerxes? Yech. Creepy."

"More androgynous than creepy."

"Androgynous *is* creepy. Men should look like men, and women should look like women."

"Says the woman with biceps and a buzz cut."

"And a C cup."

"That's true," Saul said thoughtfully, glancing at her tits. "I forgot about that."

"Well, mention it to the next blind date."

He groaned. "I can't believe you're sticking with this."

"I will *not* be the only one of us unmated at age thirty! You're eight months younger, you've got loads more time."

"You're not going to see me speed dating and fending off rapists. I'm pretty sure," he added thoughtfully. He got up. "Another beer?"

"Yeah, please. Ohhhhhhh! And the spear splits open the side of Xerxes's mouth! That's *gotta* hurt. This used to be my favorite part."

She heard the hssst! of Saul opening two more bottles. "Used to be?" he called from the kitchen.

"Now my favorite part is when the queen kills the traitor. He *did* pretty much rape her. Although she was an idiot to put herself—"

"Careful," Saul warned.

She shut up. Who was she to judge the queen's actions after what had happened last night? Saul was right, as usual.

"Why, why couldn't the spear have gone three inches to the right? Killed him dead on the spot. Although," she admitted, "that was a helluva throw.

What is he, two hundred yards away? I don't know if I could have made that throw."

She heard Saul walk toward the back of the house—probably headed for the bathroom to get rid of some beer—and stopped with the commentary.

The phone rang, and rang again. So she picked it up in time to hear Saul answer. "Hello?"

"Yeah, it's me, Darrell. Listen, I heard your friend has an STD, is that true?"

"Totally true," Saul assured him. Cain felt her mouth pop open in shock and instantly abandoned her plan to hang up.

"But . . . she's Pack, right? We don't catch stuff like that."

"It's a really nasty one. Trust me, you don't want to go anywhere near her. Things will drop off of you, I'm not kidding."

"Thanks for the heads up. I'm sure she's a nice girl and all, but who needs that shit?"

"Do me a favor," Saul the unbelievably treacherous bastard said, "and spread the word."

"Okay. Speaking of spreading the word, one of us is in the hospital—that Geoff guy?"

"Oh?" Saul asked coolly.

"Yeah, and he's yelling about suing you and your pal for assault. But nobody knows what really happened because he won't say."

"Won't he?"

"Yeah. I don't suppose you want to say."

"No," Saul said calmly. "If he wants to roll the dice, that's fine, but you might want to mention I haven't explained the full details of last night to Michael yet. But I'd be happy to. Anytime. And if he needs me to explain it in person, I'll be glad to visit him in the hospital. Anytime."

There was a pause, then Darrell said, "Like that, huh? I heard he had a rough hand with the ladies. Somebody's going to tear his throat out one of these days."

"You might have warned me before I set him up with my best friend," Saul said sharply.

"It was just a rumor. Nobody's ever said anything to Michael. There's no proof, only some talk once in a while."

"That," Saul said, "may change."

"All right. Later, guy."

"Good-bye."

Chapter 10

Saul walked back into the living room and had half a second to duck as an armchair sailed toward his head. He dodged it (barely) and it crashed into the wall behind him.

"You son of a bitch!"

"What? What? Is your beer warm?"

"This is not about the beer!" Four knickknacks arrowed toward him: a Hummel figurine, a glass unicorn, a music box, and a picture of his grandparents. Luckily, they all belonged to his late mother.

He hated glass unicorns. "And you damned well know it!"

Oh, shit.

"You, uh, heard?"

An antique end table soared through the air toward him and he sidestepped it with time to spare. Luckily, when she was pissed, her aim went to shit.

"You're telling people I have an STD?" She looked around frantically for something else to throw.

"It's for your own good," he said, his own temper rising.

"My own good?" She goggled at him, and despite the tension he couldn't help notice that her black eye had almost disappeared. *Thank God.* "How is scaring potential mates off for my own—oh my God. Oh my God! You. You! You deliberately set me up with losers and psychos and—and a rapist!"

"I didn't know Geoff would do that," he said quickly, though he was still racked with guilt, and longed to visit the hospital and take a bite out of the man's face. "I figured you wouldn't click because he's so dominant. And so are you. So I figured you'd reject him, too."

"Bastard! You're supposed to be my *friend*." She spied his keys hanging on the board, grabbed them, and threw them at him.

He snatched them out of the air and plunked them on a nearby table. "Yeah, well, maybe I'm tired of being your *friend*," he snapped.

"What? What's that supposed to mean?"

"It means, you twit, that I'm *in love with you*. It means I've been in love with you since kindergarten."

"What?" she gasped, almost wheezing.

"Didn't it occur to you that there's a reason I'm not mated yet, and it has nothing to do with our stupid pact? For Christ's sake, Cain, we were *seven* when we made that pact, did you really expect them all to stick to it? Especially Michael, who has to provide heirs?"

"You—you—"

"Then you come to me asking me to fix you up?"

"But you never said! You *never* said!"

"I only dropped a million hints, idiot!"

"Don't call me names, jackass!"

"Don't expect me to help you hook up with some random jerkoff!"

"Fine!"

"Fine!"

"I'm not staying here another minute!"

"Fine!"

"Except they towed my car this morning so I need a ride!"

"Fine!" He snatched his keys off the table and stomped toward the front door. He'd imagined this scene a thousand times, but never quite like this. In his mind, she confessed she secretly loved him, too, and they ended up in bed, and he eventually knocked her up, and they lived happily ever after.

Not this—this screaming awful fight.

Fuck.

Chapter 11

Five days later, Cain was still fuming, bewildered, and betrayed. She'd ignored Saul's calls and e-mails. She'd watched *300* nine more times.

And over and over again she thought about dates one through seven, thought about the fact that Saul had cold-bloodedly set her up with the worst Pack members he could find, men he *knew* (because he knew her as no one else did) she would find repulsive.

She hadn't thought he had it in him.

And the love thing? Ridiculous.

There was no way.

Right?

Right.

Because this was *Saul*. Sweet, stammering, beta Saul. Geeky, engineering, workaholic Saul.

Saul, who'd given her his teddy bear at age five when she'd accidentally (okay, maybe she'd lost her temper a little) ripped the head off hers.

Saul, who gave her his ice-cream cone when she dropped hers the summer they were six.

Saul, who had comforted her when her parents died the fall she was fourteen, as she had comforted him when his mother died a year later, rapidly followed by his father.

Saul, who listened impassively the spring she was seventeen when she told him about losing her virginity, then suggested she dump the guy.

And she *had*. She *had*.

Looking back through the years, she could see his subtle maneuverings, the way he always made sure she stayed single, the way he gently discouraged her from pursuing certain men, men she might have fallen for.

Sneaky treacherous bastard!

If she ever saw him again (fat chance of *that*) she would punch his face in. Repeatedly. Until he was a big bloody mess on the ground. He and Geoff the asshole could share a hospital room.

By the fifth day, she had heaved herself up off the living room couch, hosed herself off, dressed in fresh, clean clothes, and bopped down the street to the nearest bar.

She moved easily, without pain; the damage Geoff had inflicted was long gone—although she had called the Cape Cod Hospital two days ago and established he was still an inpatient. That had put the first smile on her face in seventy-two hours. She hoped his balls still hurt.

After pushing her way past the waiting crowd, after being waved in by the bouncer, she headed straight for the bar. Never had she wanted a drink so badly.

Now she was slumped on a stool, sucking down Coronas and thinking about all the ways she would mutilate Saul if she ever saw him again (fat chance of *that*).

"Excuse me?"

First, she'd break his nose. Then, she'd break out all his teeth. Then—

"Excuse me?"

She turned to look; a cute redheaded, green-eyed werewolf had slid onto the stool beside her. That was a relief; at least a monkey wasn't about to put the moves on her. "Yeah?"

"Don't I know you?"

"I dunno. Do you?"

"You're Cain, right?"

"Right." She stuck out her hand and he shook it. He really was cute, with those sparkling green eyes and that big grin. And freckles!

"I'm Darrell."

"Oh, God," she groaned, and buried her face in her hands.

Chapter 12

"I *don't* have an STD. Contrary to rumor."

"Well, that's a relief. Buy you another one?" he asked, gesturing to her beer bottle, which was almost empty.

"Sure."

"So," he said, while they were waiting for the bartender, "Saul got it wrong, huh? That's not like him."

"Oh yes it is. He got it wrong on purpose. He's been steering guys away from me for years. He just stepped it up this month."

There was an awkward pause while the bartender plunked down their drinks, then Darrell said, "Jeez, that's—uh—weird. Why would he do that?"

"Because he's gone insane?"

"I dunno, sounds like a description of a man in love to me."

"Please," she said, furiously chomping on her lime.

"That would explain," Darrell said thoughtfully, "why I also heard that you were anorexic, hooked on marijuana, and a nymphomaniac."

She nearly choked on her lime. "I haven't gotten laid in two years! And all that other stuff isn't true, either," she added belatedly.

"You're right. He *has* gone insane. Saul, of all people! Crazy over you, at least."

"Please," she said again.

"Wow," he said cheerfully, slurping his Bud. "I heard you were a little slow on the uptake, but does he have to paint it on your forehead?"

"I am not, either!" she said furiously, resisting the impulse to break the bottle over his stupid red head. "And he does not! And he *better* not. I can't believe you're on his side. Men," she snorted. "You all stick together."

"We sort of have to," he said apologetically. "Mars and Venus and all that stuff, right? Guys *have* to stick together. Otherwise, you'd destroy us all."

"That's an interesting worldview. Creepy, but interesting." She finished her beer and made up her mind. "So. You wanna go out? Tomorrow?"

"Yes," he said, "but I won't."

"Huh? Why?"

"Because Saul's in love with you and you're probably in love with him, you're just too pissed to see it. And I'm not getting in the middle of *that*. Although you are perfectly cute," he assured her.

"We're just friends," she snapped, ignoring the niggle of doubt crawling up her spine. "But thanks for the cute thing."

"No problem. But you're one hundred percent deluded about his feelings."

"Deluded?" she echoed disbelievingly.

"Oh, sure. He's totally in love with you. That's why he did all that research on every eligible male Pack member. Guy probably hasn't slept since you got back to town."

"He told me that was *work*!"

"Well, for him, it probably was."

She banged her forehead on the surface of the bar. "Jerk. Jerk. Jerk."

"Hey. Quit that." Darrell shoved his hand between her forehead and the bar, so the next time her head banged down on his hand. "Seriously, stop! You'll give yourself a concussion."

"I never *could* read his writing. I *saw* the paperwork, it was all over the living room."

"Well, you should quit bitching that you didn't have any clues. You had tons of them, sounds like."

"It's possible I hate you more than I hate Saul."

"Problem is, you *don't* hate Saul. So why don't you go see him?"

"Because he's a treacherous, lying bastard?"

"Who's been with you through—what's the phrase? Thick and thin?"

"I have just decided," she said, "that this is none of your business."

"Oh, I love to meddle. Besides, you looked so cute and forlorn I couldn't help coming over."

"Puppies are cute," she grumped. "Babies are cute. I am not cute."

"Awww, don't be so hard on yourself, cute stuff. And go see Saul!"

"Forget it."

He cupped his chin in one hand and studied her. "Man, he's a brave bastard. You'd be a handful."

"Shut up. Go away."

"If you promise to go see him, I will."

"How about if I just beat the crap out of you instead?"

"Oh, no," he said earnestly. "Then it'd be awkward if we ever ran into each other again."

"What is *with* you?"

"I'm a huge fan of true love."

Incredibly, she heard herself promise. Anything for some fucking peace and quiet.

Chapter 13

She charged into Saul's living room, having rapidly metabolized the beer and deciding to get her promise over with as soon as possible.

"All right, you treacherous son of a bitch, you sneaky sly—shit."

The house was empty. Which was weird; where *was* he at friggin' midnight, anyway? He had no life outside of work! And her! And work!

Probably out spreading more odious rumors about her; she wouldn't put it past him.

She settled down to wait. She'd wait all night if she had to. All *week*. And ooooh, she was going to give him *such* a piece of her mind, and possibly a concussion, and maybe even—

The front door swung open, and Saul staggered inside.

"Oh my God!" she cried, leaping to her feet. "What the hell happened to you?"

"Nothing," he muttered, trying to limp past her, but she blocked his way. He had a bloody nose, the beginnings of *two* black eyes, and there was something wrong with his leg.

"Sit down, let me look at your leg."

He tried to push her away and nearly fell over. She easily shoved him onto the couch, ripped his jeans open, and examined the bulge.

"Oh."

"Yeah."

"It's broken."

"Yeah."

"And it's healing really fast."

"Ye—aaaagggggghhhhhh!"

She had slammed her fist down on the bulge, straightening out the greenstick fracture with one blow.

"There!" she said with false cheer. "All fixed."

Saul leaned over the edge of the couch and threw up.

"I'll, uh, go get the mop."

"Go away," he groaned.

"Well," she replied, "normally that would be tempting, except now I have to go kill whoever beat the shit out of you. But first I have to mop up the puke."

So she went to get the mop. Thank God for hardwood floors.

Chapter 14

"So who did it?"

"I fell down the stairs."

She snorted. "How many times?"

"Look, aren't you furious with me?" He massaged his temples and winced. "What are you even doing here?"

"Sure I'm pissed. But we'll sort that out *after* I kill the guy. Which would be a lot easier if you'd give me a name. Hate to eat the wrong guy. So who was it?"

"I walked into a door."

"A door made of metal spikes?"

He groaned as she shoved a hamburger under his nose. “This thing is burned black on the outside and I just *know* it’s raw on the inside.”

“You have to eat.”

“You’re a shitty cook.”

“Well, consider it your just reward for past treacheries. Eat!”

He scowled at her, snatched the burger away, and took a big bite. He masticated for a moment, then said, “Dead cold in the middle, I knew it.”

“Shut up.” She handed him a glass of milk, and he drained it in three swallows. “Who did it?”

“I was in a car accident.”

“With how many tractor trailers?” She whipped out the washcloth and set about cleaning the blood off of his face, ignoring his efforts to push her away while he gobbled the burger.

“Cain, stop fussing, it’s been a long damn day.” He batted her hand away like it was an annoying insect.

“Saul, for Christ’s sake, will you cough up already? You—wait a minute.” She leaned forward and took a sniff. He tried to inch away from her but the couch was at his back and he had nowhere to go.

She sniffed harder. "I know that smell! That's Geoff the asshole! Oh my God! I will *kill* him! He is *dead*! So totally, stinking, fucking dead!"

"Actually, Ms. Nosy Parker, he's back in the hospital."

"Completely massively dead! Wait. What?"

"He got out today. So I went to have a chat with him about how not to treat people I've secretly been in love with for twenty-five years. He disagreed." Saul touched his left eye, puffing and a hideous greenish brown. "Vehemently. But, as the saying goes, you should see the other guy."

"You went after *that* guy? By yourself?" She threw up her hands and he flinched. "Sorry. But Jesus Christ, Saul! What has gotten *into* you this week?"

"I have no idea," he said dully.

"If you had that big a beef you should have gone to the Pack leader! Or let me handle him!"

"Ha! Not likely."

She ignored that. "Not picked a fight with someone like that. God, he could have broken your stupid *neck*."

"So? That would solve a lot of problems for you, wouldn't—aaaaggggghhhhh!"

She'd punched his bad leg again. "Now you're just sounding like a jerk. A pissed-off jerk."

"Which is," he admitted, "usually your job."

"I just cannot believe you went after him!"

"I felt guilty," he admitted. "Really, really guilty. You—I can count on one hand how many times I've seen you cry and he made you—he—y-you—and your shirt w-was all torn and he'd h-hit you a-and—a-and—"

She kissed him to shut him up.

Chapter 15

She kissed him as gently as she knew how, delicate butterfly kisses on his mouth, his cheeks, his swollen nose, his bruised eyes, his forehead, and he brought his arms around her with shocking strength and pulled her onto his lap. She gently parted his lips with her tongue and he sucked it greedily into his mouth, making her gasp.

"Wait," she said, pulling back. "Not to sound like a cocktease, which I've already been accused of this week, but you're awfully banged up. Maybe this isn't such a good—"

"Are you kidding?" he said, heaving himself off the couch with her in his arms. "And let this chance go by?" And with that he actually *ran* with her to his bedroom, dropped her on the bed, then started pulling off his clothes as quickly as possible.

"If you don't quit," she said, trying not to laugh as a sock sailed past her ear, "you're going to hurt yourself again."

"Shouldn't you be naked by now? No, wait. I want to do it."

"Bossy."

"It's been a weird week."

So she let him ease her shirt off, pull her shorts off, divest her of panties and bra. Then he was on top of her, his broad chest settling against hers as he kissed her, sucking her lips into his mouth and gently nibbling at the tender flesh. She groaned into his mouth—it *had* been two years—and arched against him when his big warm hands covered her breasts.

She ran her hands down his broad back, feeling the smooth muscles beneath the skin, praying Geoff the asshole hadn't cracked a rib or worse. She ran her fingers through his black pubic hair and grasped his cock, feeling the velvety length pulsing against her hand. He was—my, my.

"Saul, you are hung like a *horse*."

"Stop that," he groaned, "if you don't want to be done before we really get started."

"I had no *idea*."

"Please stop talking," he begged.

"Yeah, that's not really my style. It's—" He kissed her, effectively shutting her up, and she wrapped her legs around his back as he eased into her, inch by delightful inch. He was panting, harsh gasps in her ear, and moving with maddening slowness. She beat his back with her fists but he ignored her obvious urgency and sucked a nipple into his mouth.

"Saul, for Christ's sake," she groaned.

"Please s-stop talking."

"Saul, *please*!"

So he obligingly slammed into her and she screamed at the ceiling as sparks exploded in front of her eyes, as he thrust and shoved and pushed, as she tightened her grip on his hips and grabbed his ass and sank her fingernails into him.

Her orgasms were like fireworks—one, two, three, *much* better than anything she'd been achieving on her own in the last twenty-four months—and still he thrust, still he pushed inside her and withdrew and pushed again, and the sweet agony exploded through her *again* and she shrieked his name.

"Oh, God, Cain!" he cried, and then he shivered all over and she could feel him pulsing inside her, filling her up, warming her from the inside out, and she shuddered once more in answer to his pure male need.

They lay locked together, gasping.

"Oh my *God*," she said at last.

"Please don't spoil it," he murmured into her neck.

"Saul, where have you *been* all my life?"

"Wherever you've wanted me to be." Pause. "Idiot."

She laughed. "Ooooh, love the sexy pillow talk. I may melt."

"I actually don't love you; now that I've had you I think I hate you."

"Oh, you liar."

"Yeah," he sighed, and kissed her again.

Chapter 16

"Now, don't go getting a swelled head," she told him at breakfast. He'd woken her up twice in the night, once to take her from behind, once to lick every inch of her body.

He peered at her over the paper. "No, not at all."

"Just because you're the most fantastic lover ever doesn't mean I've magically fallen in love with you overnight."

"Oh, you love me," he said casually. "You're just a little slow on the uptake."

"That is just what Darrell said," she muttered.

"What?"

"Never mind. Eat your eggs, you've still got two black eyes."

"My eggs," he commented, "are runny."

"You think I cook for anybody, you ungrateful ass? Eat!"

"Runny and you put too much milk in them."

"Shut up!" she howled, and threw an English muffin at his head. He handily dodged. She tried to calm down. It was difficult, when all she wanted to do was rip his clothes off and fuck him on the kitchen table.

Saul.

Saul, of all people! Who'da thunk it?

"What I am trying to say," she managed through clenched teeth, "is that we should date."

"I was thinking more like getting married."

"Date," she continued doggedly, "and on or around my birthday, if we think it'll work out, we can get married."

"Oh." He chewed, blank-faced, then said, "I'd rather get married right now."

"You ass! Jesus, I love you." Then, horrified, she clapped a hand over her mouth. "I didn't mean it!"

"Yes, you did." He looked unbearably smug.

"It just sort of slipped out! Like—like verbal diarrhea."

"You," he said, "should write greeting cards. You've got such a way with words."

She threw another muffin at him, which he snatched out of the air and devoured in two bites. "Date!" she practically screamed. "We will date! And in two weeks, *maybe* we'll get married."

There was a polite rap on the door, and he instantly got up.

"No, stay put and eat. I'll get it. Maybe Geoff's back for round two."

"Doubt it."

She went to the front door, opened it, and saw her Pack leader, Michael Wyndham, standing on the front step.

"Cain! Congratulations!"

"Huh? I mean, good morning, Michael."

"As soon as I heard the great news I went to work."

"Huh?"

"Jeez, you're kind of slow on the uptake, aren't

you? I've got the paperwork all arranged." He handed her a sheet on thick vellum.

A marriage certificate.

And Michael, of course, was licensed to marry them.

"Saul!" she screamed, almost crumpling the license in her fist. "You—manipulative—prick!"

"Wedding day jitters?" Michael asked kindly.

"Aren't you going to invite him in?" Saul called from the kitchen.

She weighed the pleasure of slamming the door in his face against the consequences of slamming the door in his face, then grudgingly stepped aside so he could enter.

Then she trotted down the hall to the kitchen. "This doesn't prove anything! I'm not signing that thing today!"

"Well, *I* am." He was scraping the rest of his runny eggs into the garbage disposal. "You can sign it whenever you're ready."

"Which might be a long damn time, Mr. Planned Everything without Telling Me! Ever think of *that*?"

"Ticktock, Cain. You're thirty . . . when?"

"You *know* when!" she yowled.

"So," Michael said from behind her, "who's signing this thing? Say, Cain, remember that bet we made when we were just kids, about how we wouldn't get mated until we—"

She snatched the thing out of his hand. Saul handed her a pen. She signed it with an angry slash. Thrust it at her (groan) husband. Who also signed it.

"Okay," Michael said, looking at them doubtfully and taking the certificate back. "As you know, you're now legally married, but we'd love to have a formal ceremony for you at the Manor. When you're, um, not so stressed. Maybe in a week or two?"

"I'm not stressed. I'm fucking *married*."

"Well, ah, congratulations seem to be in order for the, um, happy couple."

"You bastard," she told Saul.

Her husband smiled and handed her a glass of raw eggs.

"You'll pay," she warned him. "For the next fifty years, you'll pay."

"Oh, I'm counting on it," he said, and kissed her for a lovely long time, and at one point Michael cleared his throat and left, but they didn't notice.

And now, a sneak preview of

Undead and Unworthy

the seventh installment of the
Betsy the Vampire Queen series

Chapter 1

Bored, I crossed the carpet in five steps, climbed up on Sinclair's desk, and kissed him. My left knee dislodged the phone, which hit the floor with a muffled thump and instantly started making that annoying *eee-eee-eee* sound. My right skidded on a fax Sinclair had gotten from some bank.

Surprised, but always up for a nooner (or whatever vampires called sex at 7:30 at night), my husband kissed me back with knee-weakening enthusiasm. Meanwhile, due to the aforementioned knee-skidding,

I slammed into him so hard, his chair hit the wall with enough force to put a crack in the wallpaper. More work for the handyman.

He yanked, and my (cashmere! argh) sweater tore down the middle. He shoved, and my skirt (Ann Taylor) went up. He pulled, and my panties (Target) went who-knew-where. And I was pretty busy tugging and pulling at his suit (try as I might, I could not get the king of the vampires to *not* wear a suit), so the cloth was flying.

He did that sweep-the-top-of-the-desk thing you see in movies and plopped me on my back. He reached down and I said, "Not the shoes!" so he left them alone (although I noticed the eye roll and made a mental note to bitch about it later).

He tugged, pulled, and entered. It hurt a little, because normally I needed more than sixteen seconds of foreplay, but it was also pretty fucking great (literally!).

I wrapped my legs around his waist so I could admire my sequined leopard-print pumps (don't even ask me what they cost). Then I grinned up at him, I couldn't help it, and he smiled back, his dark eyes narrow with lust. It was so awesome to be a newlywed. And I was almost done with my thank-you notes!

I let my head fall back, enjoying the feel of him, the smell of him, his hands on my waist, his dick filling me up, his mouth on my neck, kissing, licking, then biting.

Then my dead stepmother said, "This is all your fault, Betsy, and I'm not going anywhere until you fix it."

To which I replied (really quite logically), "Aaaaah! Aaaaah! AAAAAAAAAAAAHHHHHH-HHHHHHHH!"

Sinclair jerked like I'd turned into sunshine and spoke for the first time since I swept into his office. "Elizabeth, what's wrong? Am I hurting you?"

"Aaaaaaaaaaahhhhhhhhhh!"

From my vantage point, my dead stepmother was upside down, which somehow made it all the more terrible because, contrary to popular belief, you *can't* turn a frown upside down.

"You can fuss all you want, but you've got responsibilities, and don't think I don't know it." She shook her head at me and in death, as in life, her overly coiffed pineapple-blonde hair didn't move. She was wearing a fuchsia skirt, a low-cut sky blue blouse, black nylons, and fuchsia pumps. Also, too much makeup. It practically hurt to look at her. "So you better get to work."

"Aaaaaaaaaahhhhhhhhhh!"

Sinclair pulled out and started frantically feeling me. "Where are you hurt?"

"The Ant! The Ant!"

"You—what?"

Before I could elaborate (and where to begin?), I heard thundering footsteps and then Marc slammed into the closed office door. I heard him back off and grab for the doorknob, and then he was standing in the doorway. "Betsy, are you—oh my God!" He went red so fast I was afraid he was going to have a stroke. "I'm sorry, jeez, I thought that was a bad 'aaaaahhhh,' not a sex 'aaaaahhh.'"

More footsteps, and then my best friend, Jessica, was saying, "What's wrong? Is she okay?" She was so skinny and short, I couldn't see her behind Marc.

"The Ant is here!" I yowled as Sinclair assembled the rags of his suit, picked me up off the desk, and shoved me behind him. I don't know why he bothered;

Marc was gay *and* a doctor, and so couldn't care less if I was mostly naked. And Jessica had seen me naked about a million times. "Here, right now!"

"Your stepmother's in this room?" I still couldn't see her, but Jessica's tone managed to convey the sheer horror I felt at the prospect of being haunted by the Ant.

"Where *else* would I be?" the Ant, the late Antonia Taylor, said reasonably. She was tapping her Payless-clad foot and nibbling her lower lip. "What I'd like to know is, where's your father?"

"One problem at a time," I begged.

Chapter 2

After Marc decided a Valium drip probably wouldn't work on a vampire, he brought me a stiff drink instead. Which was sweet, but I was so rattled I drank it off in one gulp and it could have been paint thinner for all I knew.

"Is she still here?" he whispered.

"Of course I'm still here," my dead stepmother snapped. "I told you, I'm not going anywhere."

"I'm the only one who can hear you," I shrilled, "so just shut up!"

"Bring her another drink," Sinclair muttered. We were still in his office, but Jessica had kindly brought robes to cover our shredded clothes. "Bring her three."

"I don't need booze, I need to get rid of you-know-what."

"Very funny," the Ant grumped.

She and my father had been killed in a gruesome, stupid car accident a couple of months ago. Where she had been since her death, and why she had shown up now, I didn't know. And I didn't *want* to know. But I was going to have to find out, because the ghosts never, ever went away until I solved their little problems for them.

And where *was* my dead dad, anyway? I sighed. Non-confrontational in life, as well as in death.

"What do you want?"

"I *told* you. To fix this."

"Fix *what*?"

"*You* know."

"This is so weird," Marc murmured to Jessica, forgetting, as usual, about superior vamp hearing. "She's having a conversation with the chair."

"She is not, quiet so I can hear."

"I don't know," I said, "I really, really don't. Please tell me."

"Stop playing games."

"I'm *not*!" I almost screamed. Then I felt Sinclair's soothing hands on my shoulders and sagged into him. Like our honeymoon hadn't been stressful enough, what with all the dead kids and Marc and Jessica crashing it and all. This was a hundred times worse.

"If you could just—" I began, when the office door crashed open, nearly smashing into Marc, who yelped and jumped aside.

Garrett, the Fiend formerly known as George, stood in the doorway, panting. Since he was seventy-some years old and didn't need to breathe, I knew at once something was seriously fucked.

"They're awake," he gasped. "And they want to kill you."

"Who?" Sinclair, Jessica, Marc, and I asked in unison.

"The other Fiends. I've been feeding them my blood and they're pissed. They—they sort of 'woke up' and now they want to kill you."

"It's this lifestyle you lead," the Ant said smugly. "These things are bound to happen."

"Oh, shut the fuck up!" I barked. I actually had to clutch my head; which problem to tackle first?

"You'd better sit down and tell us everything," Sinclair said, reminding me he was the vampire king. Bam. Decision made. We'd deal with what Garrett had done first.

So take that, dead stepmother.